THE PIE SISTERS

A Novel By
Leigh Brown & Victoria Corliss

With a few notable exceptions, the characters, places, and events in this story are fictional and completely of our own creation.

This book is dedicated to Lake Canandaigua, New York, and Mousam Lake, Maine. Special places with special memories.

*   *   *

Acknowledgements

The *Pie Sisters* is a fictional story born of our own personal memories and experiences summering on lakes. Toasting marshmallows over a bonfire, July 4th fireworks, and family game nights, are just a few of the special moments we have enjoyed and will always hold dear. We are two very lucky girls.

We want to thank Jennifer Cournoyer, our editor, for her important role in bringing *The Pie Sisters* to life. Your respect for and keen interest in the story equaled our own deep affection for the Lane sisters and their adventures. Thank you so much.

Though we pride ourselves on being multi-taskers, we were at times consumed by our enthusiasm for this novel. Hours of writing often turned into days. Meals went uncooked. Laundry piled up. Errands were forgotten. To our husbands and sons, we offer you our heartfelt apologies, and infinite thanks. Your support and love mean everything to us.

Last, but not least, to our own real-life siblings for keeping the bonds of friendship strong. Family first and forever.

PROLOGUE

Applause erupts from the audience as scholars, researchers, students, even a few local politicians stand and cheer for Professor Natalie Lane. She blushes with pride.

They are cheering for my mother. Her spellbinding lecture on "The Work of Women" has them as captivated as a group of school children at story hour.

Well, at least it's almost over. Crossing my fingers, I pray that the post-lecture 'mix and mingle' will be over soon too. It is late, and the stuffy auditorium is hot. My neck is sweaty and itchy where the collar of my wool cardigan scratches against it. Wiggling uncomfortably in my seat, I check to see how my sisters Shelby and Lily are holding up.

Shelby sits on my left, posting guard in the aisle seat while my mother gives her lecture. Her posture is perfect, but for a slight rounding of her shoulders as she buries her nose in a book. At nine years old, Shelby is the oldest of the Lane girls. That's what our parents' friends and colleagues always call us, The Lane Girls, as if we come in a packaged set or something. Hardly. We barely look alike. We're not even the same age. And if we are being totally honest, sometimes I don't even *like* my sisters.

Little Miss Perfect Shelby is my parents' favorite. I mean, what's not to love about a kid who gets herself up and ready for school every day, dragging me along in the process? While Mom and Dad compare schedules, figuring out who has school drop-off and pick-up, Shelby efficiently pours cereal into two bowls and splashes them with milk. She hands one to me before neatly digging into her own. After school, it is more of the same. She fixes us a nutritious snack like apples with peanut butter. Just once I would love to break Mom's no-junk-food rule and have a Milky Way bar or a handful of Fritos before we start our homework.

Shelby has the neatest handwriting I have ever seen. You could take a ruler to the letters; they are that straight. In third grade, she even won a penmanship award. I am pretty sure she is gunning for a repeat this year. Sometimes, when she has her 'focused face' on, I sneak out of the room to watch TV, but she always catches me. Shelby has eyes in the back of her head and can do many things at once. Dad calls her his Little Multi-tasker.

I call her Drill Sergeant. "You're not the boss of me!" I yell as she pushes me up the stairs to bed. "Mom!" But my mother is busy covering my little sister Lily in a pink cotton nightgown with flowers and butterflies patterned all over it. She smiles gratefully at Shelby, and I know the battle is lost.

"Thank you all so much for coming."

As the lecture ends, Shelby lifts her head, a far away look clouding her large gray eyes. With a sigh, she closes her book, smoothing the wrinkles from her blouse as she tucks her shoulder-length auburn hair securely behind both ears. Shelby's unconscious movements remind me of Mrs. Patterson, our head school librarian. Mrs. P. has a habit of fussing uncomfortably with her clothes as she rattles off an endless list of rules: "Whisper voices only. Walk don't run. Raise your hand if you have a question." She's kind of quirky, but clearly in charge.

"Time to go, Yeardley. Wake Lily, please." With sure hands, Shelby begins fastening the buttons on her coat. In a minute, she will do the same for our sister. Just like a little mother.

I turn to my right where five-year-old Lily is sleeping. Snuggled deep into the auditorium's red velvet seat, one tiny thumb corks her rosebud mouth. Lily's soft blonde hair frames her cherubic face. Her crystal blue eyes open suddenly, as I give her belly a gentle 'wake up' poke. She giggles. "Adorable," my mom calls her. That is why she is my parents' other favorite daughter.

I was only two when Lily was born. Mom and Dad brought her home from the hospital, a tiny caterpillar cocooned in a fluffy pink swaddling blanket. Now, she is a little girly girl who loves dresses, shiny things, and rainbows. At Christmastime, when she is dressed up like a china doll, I think she would make a great angel for the top of our tree.

Even though she is the baby of the family, Lily has her own room across the hall from our parents. It is painted lavender with unicorns prancing across the walls. A child-size canopy bed that reminds me of a puffy cloud floats in the middle of the room. The Princess Room, Shelby and I call it, incredibly glad that it is not our room. Our room has pale blue walls, matching twin cherry wood beds, and windows that look out to the backyard sandbox and swing set. It is not the slightest bit frou- frou. That would never do for such a sensible person as Shelby or a tomboy like me.

I am the second child of Professors Natalie and Thomas Lane. I am a favorite daughter too. Dad says I'm "The Hub" because I am smack dab in the middle between Shelby and Lily. Mom says I'm the heart of the family because she says I feel things more deeply than the rest of them.

I don't know about that last part. But, I am a lot like both of my parents. I have Dad's easy-going temperament, and Mom's unusual copper-flecked gold eyes. I also share their talent for problem solving. I spend a lot of time thinking about important stuff like building the best Dodge Ball team for recess, and who I'm going to trade snacks with at lunchtime. Carrot sticks for potato sticks is a tough sell for most people, but not me. I have a knack for accentuating the positive, especially at home.

At home, my parents listen intently as Shelby tells them about her day at school; how she helped her teacher run the video machine when its technical complexities had the teacher stymied, and how she got an A on the math test she had studied for so diligently. Shelby just loves school.

Not me. Before anyone can ask, I tactfully change the subject. "Mr. Gronkowski says I'm the fastest girl in gym class. I'm even faster than Bobby Taylor, and he's a boy!"

Satisfied that I have diverted any possible interest in my schoolwork progress while capturing their undivided attention, I understate the obvious. "It's no big deal really." My pretense of nonchalance and humility is Oscar-worthy, I think.

"Lily!" My parents and Shelby jump as a unit to rescue my baby sister as spilt milk splashes in front of her. The princess laughs, delighted with all the fuss and excitement. And just like that, the spotlight shifts off of me.

"Yeardley, go get some paper towels, please. Quickly, before little Princess Lily here becomes a milk-soaked sponge."

"Sponge!" The center of attention shrieks, mimicking my mother, and they all laugh. For college professors, my parents sure can be dumb sometimes. But mostly they are very smart. Mom is a professor in the study of women, gender, and sexuality at Harvard University in Cambridge. Dad teaches engineering at Boston University.

Usually, they take their own cars to work from our house in Wellesley. But sometimes, they drive together, and that makes them very happy. From the back seat, with Shelby and Lily on either side of me, I watch as Dad gets set to back down the driveway.

"You girls ready?" he asks, laying an arm across the back of my mother's seat and twisting slightly.

Out on the road he reclaims his outstretched arm and takes hold of Mom's knee with his hand. She gives his hand a squeeze, and smiles back at him. Moments like that make me feel good because then I know Mom and Dad won't be lonely without us this summer when we go visit our Aunt Nola.

They can't come with us because "We'll be working, doing research," they explained. "But you'll have so much fun living with Aunt Nola at the lake. I bet you won't even miss us."

They look a little worried about that, so we rush to assure them otherwise. "We will! We will!" my sisters and I shout, wrapping our arms around their legs and squeezing like a giant python.

Secretly, I am a little excited. Eight whole weeks of living on a lake where we can swim and play and hunt for crawfish. That's what Aunt Nola said, although none of us has ever been to her house before. It is the same house my mom and her big sister grew up in.

Mom says it is so beautiful there we won't ever want to come home. Dad says we had better, or he'll have to throw us over his shoulders and carry us back. No matter how much fun we're having, no matter how much junk food Aunt Nola lets us eat.

Did he just wink at me?

THE LETTER

Shelby climbed the red brick steps of her Brooklyn home, a menu for dinner forming in her head; something cool and quick, but still filling for Matt. She headed towards the mailbox, grabbing the contents tucked inside it. Still thinking about dinner, Shelby shuffled mindlessly through the mail, stopping short at a letter addressed to her. There was no mistaking the elegant cursive that spelled out her name, or the return address in the upper left corner of the envelope. *Aunt Nola!*

Shelby had not spoken to her aunt in a while. She gave herself a mental kick. *What's wrong with you, how could you be so thoughtless?* She had been busy, working and moving in with Matt. Still, it was no excuse. "It won't happen again," she promised, staring at the letter in her hand. At least she had remembered to send Nola her new address.

Too excited to go inside, Shelby sat on the steps and opened the envelope. The last time she had spoken to Nola, Shelby thought the conversation had seemed a little strained. It was totally unlike Nola, who almost always turned a quick catch-up call into an animated hour-long investigation of Shelby's life. But

9

that day, Nola had kept it short and sweet. A feeling of unease crept over Shelby. Was Nola okay?

With the letter still folded in her hand, Shelby thought about the summers she and her sisters had spent with Aunt Nola at her home on Canandaigua Lake. It was another world to them, even though their mom and Nola had both been born and raised there. Natalie, the more audacious of the two, had left for college and never looked back. Nola, the homebody, had stayed. It was Nola who had introduced Shelby and her sisters to their new summer stomping grounds.

"Canandaigua means 'The Chosen Spot,' " Nola had told them years ago. And Shelby knew why. It was the only place in the world where she felt like a kid. "You're too young to be so mature," Nola had chided her gently. "You'll be grown before you know it, Shelby, sweetheart. Just have fun while you're here. You know how, don't you?"

With Nola's help, she had quickly learned. Stomping barefoot in rain puddles, she had felt the mud oozing between her toes. She had clambered through rocky gorges like a monkey on a tree, her hair whipping lightly across her face. Free from its usual tidy ponytail, the ends tickled her nose and made her laugh. At the lake, every day was an adventure and the unexpected happened on a regular basis. Hands down, they were the best summers of her life.

She unfolded the beautiful ecru stationary with Nola's monogram, *NHA*, gracing the top of the page in deep blue letters.

Dearest Shelby,

It has been a long time, too long, since you and your sisters last visited. The lake and I both miss you. You may not know it, but this summer I will be turning sixty-five. My birthday wish this year is for all of my nieces to be here with me, to celebrate.

Just think, one week together at the lake. It would be like old times. I know it's asking a lot, but I hope you will come and be a part of the lake again for as long as you can. One thing I have learned in my nearly sixty-five years, is that we can't predict what the future will bring or how much time we have to enjoy it.

Love and kisses,

Aunt Nola

Tears dropped on the expensive stationary, staining it with watermarks. Shelby wiped them away, sniffing at her silliness. *Why the tears, girl?* Nola's invitation was a good thing. Like Nola said, it had been too long since Shelby had visited her at the lake. What better way to escape the blistering heat of New York City in mid-July?

Scooping the rest of the mail off the step, Shelby reached for the door, already planning her trip. First order of business, call Yeardley and Lily.

* * *

Several states away, in Massachusetts, Yeardley was finishing up her day at Cooper Ltd., a bag of Doritos and a large glass of Pinot Grigio foremost on her mind. It was Tuesday, and *Real Housewives of Somewhere* was on tonight. She couldn't wait to see who would get into a catfight this week.

The office had pretty much emptied out by the time Yeardley readied to leave. Opening the bottom drawer of her desk, she pulled out her purse. The face of her phone was dark, but she checked it anyway for text or voicemail messages. Nothing. Disappointed, she slung her bag over her shoulder, and headed home.

Twenty minutes later, Yeardley drove her baby blue Sonata into the parking lot of her Watertown apartment complex. She parked, and walked briskly across the scorching asphalt expanse, towards the four-story red brick building she called home. It was hard to believe she had lived here almost three years already, with little to show for it. Home was a one-bedroom apartment filled with cast-off furniture from her parents' house. She had never felt settled enough to invest in her own stuff. And money was always a little tight.

Yeardley held two jobs; one at a local coffee shop, the other, a new office position at Cooper Ltd. Neither one was her dream job, but they paid the bills. Years ago, she had thought of becoming a nurse, or maybe a teacher, something that involved helping people. But those professions required more training and education than interested her. Besides, book smarts weren't everything. According to her dad, she had instinct and resolve guiding her. One of these days maybe she would figure out exactly what that meant.

Inside the lobby, the building's mailboxes were a steel wall of uniform rectangles distinguished by resident names and apartment numbers. Yeardley unlocked her box, pulling out the two envelopes tucked inside. She flipped through them, praying they weren't bills. Spotting Aunt Nola's return address, she slammed the box shut and dashed upstairs to read in private.

Nola's words jumped off the page. "....have you all here....to be part of the lake again." How long had it been? She snorted. *Don't act like you don't know.* Had it really been ten years? *Since I last saw him?* Feeling warm, she turned the AC on and read the letter again.

Nola's timing was perfect, as if she had a sixth sense. Tired from work, Yeardley settled on the couch, stretching her long legs on the coffee table in front of her. One week, huh? Well, she never could say no to Nola. And she wasn't about to start now.

*   *   *

Two thousand miles away, the sun shone brightly, warming the aqua shores of Miami. South Beach was covered with girls in bikinis and guys in swim trunks all vying for each other's attention. Like New York, Miami was a city that never slept, only hotter.

At Alvarez Designs, Lily was sharing laughs with some of her coworkers, and celebrating nearly four years of employment at one of *the* top design firms in the United States. A graduate of the Rhode Island School of Design, she had always dreamed of being an interior designer, but New England's brutal winters were not for her. So before the ink had even dried on her diploma, Lily had pointed her compass to the warmest place she could think of, and set course for Miami.

Settling quickly into her new home, she had landed her new job almost as fast. Lily's beauty was hard to ignore and she had learned early on how to use her good looks to her advantage. Within a few weeks, Lily had landed a position with Alverez Designs, advancing quickly from design assistant to full time designer.

Lily liked to credit her critical eye and vivacious personality for much of her success. Clients loved her. She supposed it didn't hurt either that she was sleeping with her boss and the company owner, Diego Alverez. A swarthy Cuban, Diego was nearly flawless. A successful forty-something with a body to rival that of a twenty-year-old, he was the most sophisticated man Lily had ever met. And when Lily and Diego stepped out together, people stared at them like they were Hollywood celebrities.

Lily had to admit, she loved the attention Diego showered on her, but sometimes working with her lover was complicated. Though her coworkers never said anything to her face, Lily knew they gossiped about all the plumb assignments she landed; never crediting her talent for any of them. Lily's best friend in the office, Carolina, would sometimes share a snarky comment that she had overheard.

"Lisa said that Brett Mullins actually requested her for his bachelor pad redesign, but somehow you ended up on the account."

"She's full of shit!" Lily seethed. "Brett spoke directly to Diego. No one was requested. Diego decided to put me on the account because things had gone so well with Mikey Gonsalves. And since they're teammates, Diego thought Brett would be more comfortable with me. Honestly, Lisa's such a bitch."

"Don't pay her any attention. She's just jealous. You're a damned good designer. Lisa knows that. She just doesn't like that she's your support staff on that project. Lisa thinks it's beneath her," Carolina said as she pulled fabric samples off a nearby chair and gestured for Lily to sit down.

"Carolina, I'm starting to feel like I'm always going to be Diego's girlfriend first. I've paid my dues here, you know. I was staying until all hours of the day and night in the beginning and doing the grunt work just like everyone else."

"People are going to talk as long as you and Diego are together. You just have to decide if you are going to let it bother you." Carolina shot Lily a knowing look. "There's no reason why you can't mix business with pleasure. Just be sure that you are getting what you want out of both."

"Hmmm..." Lily replied. "I have to tell you that I'm starting to think that working and being in a relationship with Diego is never going to be okay with everyone else here. Maybe something has to give."

Carolina looked puzzled. "What are you thinking? Leaving Diego, or leaving Alverez Designs?"

"I'm not sure I want to leave either. But I'm feeling like I just need a little more...something...respect? Validation? I think I'm good designer on my own, not just as Diego's employee."

"You are good!" Carolina agreed. "But think about it, Lily. Diego has the best design firm in southern Florida. He lands all the best accounts. You know you love a client who has an unlimited budget! Are you ready to give all that up to strike out on your own?"

"Well, Carolina, that's the $64,000 question," Lily replied.

Today, Lily still didn't have an answer to that question. Right now she had other things on her mind. "Sorry," Lily apologized to her coworkers. "I've got to run." It was almost time for her to be sitting front and center at the fashion event of the season. "Chantal is debuting her resort wear collection at Grove Galleries. I promised I'd be there for moral support."

With a quick wave, Lily headed for the door, juggling her oversized Prada bag and leather briefcase. Piling them unceremoniously into the back seat of her Mercedes C300, a recent gift from Diego, she glanced quickly at the diamond encrusted Rolex wrapped around her wrist. Another gift from Diego, it said she had just enough time to stop and freshen up before the show.

Lily navigated the crowded city streets like a pro. Deftly avoiding the rush hour traffic jams and hordes of tourists, she made her way swiftly to Diego's Miami Tower high-rise home. Like everything else he owned it was gorgeous. Lily adored every inch of that apartment, all the 3,200-square-feet-of-pure-luxury-design of it. And to her delight, Diego loved having her there, too.

Nola's letter topped the stack of mail Diego's housekeeper had left for them on the hall table. Lily paused briefly, the sight of Nola's handwriting bringing back memories of her aunt's daily grocery lists and menus. Not to mention chore lists with each of the sisters' names assigned to at least one, but never more than two tasks a day.

"All work and no play will make my beautiful girls very, very dull," Nola would laugh. Lily chuckled softly as she opened the letter.

A celebration. Instantly, Lily was back at the lake, sitting by a bonfire making s'mores. It was the 4th of July, and a perfect day of swimming and barbecuing with neighbors was coming to a close. Fireworks shot brilliantly across the night sky, and to Lily, flopped on the soft grass, her eyes turned toward the heavens, it looked as though the stars were parting, making way for the flashes of color streaking through them. Magical. That was the only way to describe it, to describe all of their summers with Nola at the lake. Miami may have heat and excitement, but it had nothing on Shepardsville and Canandaigua Lake.

"Canandaigua, here I come." And with that, Lily headed for her closet.

SHELBY

A puff of warm air drifted into the kitchen where I was chopping tomatoes with practiced precision. The pseudo breeze felt like hot breath on my sticky skin. Man, I could not wait to get to the lake. Yeardley, Lily, and I used to spend countless hours cooling ourselves in Canandaigua's refreshing waters. Afterwards, we would look like prunes with our shriveled skin and blue lips. At the lake, even the hottest days felt good.

Scraping the tomatoes from the cutting board into a salad bowl, I grabbed a carrot, and started dicing. Matt would be home from his run soon, if he didn't get heatstroke first. Running in these hot temperatures could not be healthy. Briefly, I considered bringing him with me to the lake. He could run to his heart's content there. Just as quickly, the thought vanished from my mind. This was going to be a girls-only week.

I had broken the news of Aunt Nola's birthday to him while we were riding the subway home from work one day, "She wants me and the girls to come celebrate. She's turning sixty-five."

Packed in the subway car like a tin full of smelly sardines, I could hardly wait to get out; out of the city where we both work as project managers at a tech firm, and out of Brooklyn, our new home.

Don't get me wrong. I have an incredible life, the life I have always wanted. I have a solid career, a nice home, a great guy. Matt is the only guy I know who is as smart and kind and loving as my dad. And just like Dad, I can always count on Matt to be a voice of reason. I do not often need a sounding board, but it is nice to know he is there if and when I do.

We met at work, in the elevator. It was my first day and I wanted everything to be perfect. Intent on checking for lint on my slacks, I barely noticed him standing next to me. He looked about my age, and was tall, maybe six feet, with a tidy mop of thick dark hair. His large hands were frantically attempting to straighten his tie, or possibly make a noose. It was hard to tell which.

"Is it your first day?" I asked, my question bringing his hands to a sudden halt.

"Is it that obvious?" he asked, taking the opportunity to give me his own once-over.

My hands moved self-consciously under his gaze, smoothing away non-existent creases in my clothes. I hoped he liked what he saw. My favorite navy blue pantsuit was a perfect first-day-of-work choice. It flattered without accentuating the few curves my trim body actually possessed. I was wearing matching pumps that added a good two inches to my natural born five foot six. Tall and slim and nervous as hell, that was me. Tucking a strand of hair behind one ear I waited anxiously for his opinion.

"You too?" Unfazed by my blank stare, he spoke again, slowly, in case I didn't understand English. "Is it your first day, too?"

I nodded, trying to remember my words. "I hate first days, don't you?"

The elevator doors opened before he could answer. I moved forward, squaring my shoulders as I went. *This is it, Shelby, showtime.* I glanced at Matt, who was giving a final tug to his tie.

"Don't worry," I said. "It will be over soon. Before you know it, we'll be running this place ourselves." Full of bravado, I stepped off the elevator, "You coming?"

We've been together ever since, splitting our time between my apartment and his, until one day last year, Matt suggested we get a place together.

"It doesn't make sense for us to be paying rent for two places. Let's just move in together, okay?"

"Okay." It wasn't a terribly romantic proposition, but that's Matt. He is an expert in logic and reason. I love that about him.

So we found a reasonably spacious duplex on a quiet, tree-lined street in the Park Slope section of Brooklyn, and moved in together. Our new place is great. It's close to Prospect Park, where Matt can go running or we can take walks by the lake if we want. It's close to several subway lines and not far at all from the bars and restaurants on Fifth and Seventh avenues. Living here makes me feel like such an adult.

No more post-college sharing of tiny apartments with too many girls, just to make it affordable. No more heaving and hefting giant loads of laundry to the laundromat six blocks away, in the pouring rain. I am a grown woman now with an aspiring career and excellent salary. I am one half of an adult relationship with a mature man, living in my first real grown-up home. I am living the dream. What more could a girl ask for?

Marriage definitely. Children someday. It will happen, eventually. I know it as surely as I know every contour of Matt's face; the little dimple in his chin, the smile lines that fan from the corners of his hazel eyes, the parallel lines that form between his brows when he's working on a particularly tough crossword puzzle or competing in one of his weekly basketball games. I know because Matt is The One. And when the time is right, we will make the move to marriage and family; but not before, because Matt and I are both smart about these things. We don't ever leap before looking. Unlike Yeardley, who always seems to be flying by the seat of her pants, hoping for the best; or Lily, banking on her beauty and charm to get what she wants. It makes me shudder just thinking about living that way.

"Hey." Back from his evening run, Matt swooped in, kissing my proffered cheek.

"Gross! You're all sweaty." Handing him a towel to mop the sweat from his bare chest and arms, I scolded him. "You know, you really shouldn't run in this heat. It's not healthy."

"Probably not," he agreed, "but if I'm going to be in shape for that half marathon in October, what choice do I have?"

"Really? That's months away. I thought you were supposed to be smart."

"Smart enough to hydrate and pace myself." He gestured proudly to his lean runner's body. "This temple didn't build itself, you know." Matt swiped a carrot from the cutting board and took a bite. "Now, if you'll excuse me, there's a shower calling my name."

Matt headed for the bedroom, waving the orange vegetable with flourish, while I returned to the tasks at hand. Besides making dinner, I was compiling a mental list of meals to leave for Matt while I was at the lake. Clearly, the man needed looking after. But time at the lake, with Nola and my sisters, is something I need.

Canandaigua was my home away from home. I closed my eyes letting my senses take over, summoning the smells and feeling of being at the lake. Cool water lapping at my toes as they dangled from the wooden dock; quiet hours sitting on the worn planks, reading to my heart's content, mindless of the time. There were no schedules at the lake, only carefree days that flowed into star-filled nights of chasing fireflies and catching them in Aunt

Nola's pickling jars. In the morning, when the sun rose, the smell of bacon and blueberry pancakes would waft from the kitchen below my room, calling me to breakfast and another perfect day.

"Hey!"

At the sound of Matt's voice, my eyes snapped to attention, pulling me back to the present. Matt waved his hand in front of my face.

"Shelby? Did you hear me?"

"Sorry, just daydreaming. What did you say?"

Freshly showered and smelling great, Matt handed me a glass of chilled white wine. Grabbing his own glass off the counter he took a sip and asked, "How was work today?"

Matt and I worked for the same company but in different departments. Aside from the occasional cross-over project that required expertise from both of our teams, we rarely saw each other during the business day.

"Good," I answered. "Now that OAR is behind us. I thought that project was going to be the death of me, but it looks like I'll live to see another day."

Matt agreed. "You had your hands full with that one, that's for sure. On the bright side, you showed everyone what a superstar you really are. If that doesn't get the attention of the guys up top, I don't know what will."

"From your lips to God's ears. Before I leave for the airport tomorrow, I'll check my email and voice messages one more time, in case there are any last details I need to take care of. Then I can relax and enjoy my vacation."

Drizzling olive oil and lemon juice over the salad, I tossed it lightly and handed the bowl to Matt. "Take that to the table, would you?" Wiping my hands on a dishtowel, I joined him.

"I wish I could take you to the airport, but the boys and I have a training clinic for our run."

"Not a problem." I would be fine. He was the one I was worried about. "Are you sure you're going to be okay while I'm gone?"

"I'll be fine. I've got my routine: work, running, Wednesday night baseball league, TV Thursday line up. You know the drill."

That I did. "Excellent. Then I won't worry about you." *Or anything at all.* "Now let's eat. I still have food to prep for your meals while I'm gone. Then I need to pack."

Not that there was much to pack. Dress code at the lake was casual: shorts, t-shirts and flip-flops. The nights could get cool sometimes, so I'd throw in a pair of sweats too, and warmer pajamas, just in case. I would need one nice outfit in case we did something special. Everything I needed would fit perfectly in a carry-on bag. When I landed at Rochester International Airport, I could bypass baggage claim and head straight to the rental car counter.

"I'll make the reservation," I had offered my sisters, assuming responsibility for booking and paying for the car. When Yeardley and Lily got there, we could all jump in and go. Let the fun begin.

YEARDLEY

"Thanks, Mom. I owe you one." I owed her a whole lot more than that, but who's counting? My parents worry about me. I am not grounded like Shelby or determined like Lily. They both see the big picture and go after it. I live in the present, keeping my sights on the here and now. What good is the future if you're asleep the whole way there?

I know this irritates Shelby to no end. She would never leave anything to chance, always counting on her alphabetically organized to-do lists, daily planners, and personal finance charts to keep her on track. Lily, on the other hand, doesn't seem to care what I do. Or what anyone else does for that matter. Ever since she moved to Miami, she has been living life large, staying in touch sporadically. But she is happy and thriving, and that's good enough for Mom and Dad.

I'm happy too, sort of. I'm just a little worried that this is it. That I'm twenty-seven years old and my best years are already behind me.

"There's an expression," Nola once told me. "Somewhere in the middle lies the truth." We were at the lake, of course, because almost everything important that has happened in my life, happened at the lake. We were sitting on the porch swing, swaying in easy unison as Nola enjoyed her "happy hour," pre-dinner cocktail. She had one every night, usually a lime gimlet, or a sweet Manhattan, but sometimes her drink of choice was a thirst-quenching beer straight out of the bottle. It depended on her mood. Tonight it was a Manhattan loaded with maraschino cherries that bobbed up and down as she tipped her glass.

This was my favorite time of day, gliding with Nola on the swing, gazing at the sun-dappled lake. Nightfall was still a couple of hours away. Plenty of time to soak up the last rays of sunshine before evening's cool temps sent us scurrying for sweatshirts and jeans. "I don't get it," I told her, resting my head on her shoulder for support, and to hide my guilty expression.

Nola laughed. "Oh, Yeardley, you're a terrible liar and you know it. Something's going on with you and Jackson. Something big." With a gentle nudge, she lifted my head and bestowed one of her all-knowing looks upon me. But I was having none of it.

"You're crazy, Aunt Nola. Nothing's going on, everything is fine."

"Then why have you been walking around like the weight of the world is on your shoulders, hmm? You're worried about something, and it's obvious you're trying to figure it out. You're not invisible, you know."

That right there was why I loved her so much. Only one other person knew me as well. I felt awful not telling her, but I couldn't, not this time. This was way too personal. "Honestly, Aunt Nola, I'm fine, I promise." Planting a kiss on her cheek, I met her probing stare with a concentrated look of innocence. "Promise."

Nola shrugged, sipping her drink in surrender. The inquisition was over. Thank God. I stood up feeling the need to do something nice for her like set the dinner table when it wasn't even my turn. Nola spoke again.

"Somewhere in the middle lies the truth, and you're the middle, Yeardley. You are your own truth. Not Shelby, or Lily, or your parents, or me. Please remember that, honey." I nodded, pretending her words made sense before escaping into the house.

The truth is, I don't know what I am doing. I work two jobs; one as the executive assistant to the finance director of a small investment firm. It makes me feel quasi professional and pretty smart. My other job is at a Starbucks around the corner from my apartment. I'm a barista. I love this job, getting to know new customers and chatting up the regulars. I know what they like and I have their orders ready and waiting for them when they come in. It makes them feel special which makes me feel good.

Also, unlike my sisters, I don't have a boyfriend, at least not at present. I've had boyfriends, of course. I haven't always been single. My friends tell me I am pretty. I credit this to my parents, and to swimming several times a week at the Y. It keeps me toned and lean. The chlorine has tinted my brown hair a soft shade of shiny caramel that streaks blonde in the summer. People tell me it brings out the amber in my eyes.

I am not an optimist like Lily or pragmatic like Shelby, but somewhere in between the two. I am a realist, taking one day at a time and trying to make the most of it. Like Nola said, 'we can't predict what the future will bring,' so why kill ourselves trying?

Maybe a week at the lake was all I needed, a trip back to the last place I remember knowing exactly what I wanted and going after it. I was a different person at the lake, happy and confident. And not just me, Shelby and Lily were different there too. We were all transformed by the magical powers of 'The Chosen Spot.' I couldn't get back there fast enough.

Thanks to Mom and Dad, I would be getting there faster now that I didn't have to drive the six hours to Shepardsville.

"Consider it an early birthday gift," Mom urged when I tried to refuse their generous offer of a plane ticket. "And think how much fun it will be meeting up with your sisters at the airport and driving to Nola's together."

My birthday wasn't until September, but Mom had a knack for tact. We both knew I couldn't afford to buy my own ticket. Gifting me one made us both feel better. And much as I hated to admit it, it did sound fun: the Lane Girls together once again.

"Well, when you put it that way, and *only* because it's a birthday gift," I accepted graciously. "Thanks, Mom, I owe you one."

LILY

The sun was high in the sky, heating my skin to an uncomfortable level. I knew it was time to let my backside have a turn, but I was feeling particularly lazy in the thick padded chaises at Miami Towers. They circled the large, kidney-shaped pool in pairs, beckoning residents to relax in their decadent luxury. "First come, first served" the pool signs read, but I had never had a problem snagging one, any time of day.

Sitting alone, I still could not believe Diego had refused to join me. He was such an old man sometimes. He didn't want any more wrinkles, he said. For Christ's sake, he's Cuban not Irish! Well, it was his loss, preserving himself in the air-conditioned apartment instead of spending time with me in my skimpy crocheted bikini.

Taking a sip of my sparkling water, I drizzled some more sunscreen on my shoulders. Diego's method seemed extreme to me, but I knew how important it was to protect my skin from burning. The Miami Melody Ball was tonight, and I needed to look perfect.

A pale blue Versace dress was waiting for me in my closet. It was from Donatella's recent spring collection. Diego had insisted I buy it even though I have a closet full of gorgeous clothes. He spoils me beyond belief. Whatever I want, whether I need it or not, Diego gives it to me, showering me with gifts and compliments. And I love being pampered. We make a perfect pair.

I was thriving in Miami. I loved the heat. I loved the constant excitement even more.

"You have the attention span of a gnat," Shelby often told me. "You're such a dreamer, Lily. You need to focus more."

She's kind of right. But my need for constant change is also part of why I love my job so much. Every few months, I have a new project with a different set of faces. It keeps things interesting. Not to mention the clientele. I work hard at filling my client roster with Miami's premier athletes, renowned artists, and world-class entertainers. It's not just my job it's my passion.

I've been thinking about this a lot lately, Shelby's advice ringing in my ears. At twenty-five, I am leading a pretty charmed life. I know it. And I know how lucky I am to have Diego. But that nagging feeling of wanting more for me is like an itch that cannot be scratched. I just can't shake the urge to strike out on my own. Didn't Carolina always say that my clients were the most satisfied in the office? I wonder, what it would be like if I really put myself to the test. Could I make it work?

Maybe a week at the lake is exactly what I need. Spending time with Aunt Nola and my sisters, remembering my summers as a kid. Who knows? Perhaps they would have some insight on what I should do. My phone rang, somewhere in the bottom of my Tory Burch beach bag. Caught up in my thoughts, I let it ring. Whoever it was could leave a message.

Moments later, the phone beeped. I sighed, shifting in my chaise, and grabbed my pink crystal-studded smart phone. It was a text from Shelby.

Booked a rental car. Meet me and Y at the airport Hertz counter. Don't forget: swimsuit, comfortable shoes and a hat. Don't want your fair skin to burn.

Did she forget I live in Miami? I chuckled at Shelby, in charge, as usual. Just once, I would love to see her let go and relax. I stood up, gathering my bag and beach towel around me. We would all be at the lake soon enough. But right now, it was time to show Miami what Princess Lily from New England was all about.

SATURDAY

THE ARRIVAL

The afternoon sun nearly blinded Shelby as she looked both ways before crossing through the intersection. Using her directional, she turned left onto the familiar dirt road that was 32nd Street Loop. A few more minutes and they would be pulling into Nola's driveway.

"I remember the first time I ever drove this road myself," she recalled, capturing her sisters' undivided attention. "Nola was teaching me to drive so I could take my test when we got back home. I was so scared. But I did okay, if I do say so myself."

"You'd be the only one to say so."

From the passenger seat, Yeardley could not resist teasing her. "I still can't believe Nola risked all of our lives by making me and Lily ride with a rookie at the wheel."

Shelby scowled fiercely. Yeardley repented. "On the other hand, you were always a very conscientious driver. Still are."

She glanced at Shelby, her hands glued to the steering wheel, precisely at 10:00 and 2:00. Darting frequent glances to the rearview mirror, Shelby looked just like a student driver. Yeardley turned away, hiding her smile.

"Hey, guys, look."

From the back seat, Lily pointed to the road ahead of them. Excitement lit up her face as Shelby powered the rental car up the gradually inclining road toward its flattened peak.

"Wait for it," Lily murmured, and the girls held their collective breath. For all of their differences, in this one thing they were united: the awe-inspiring first sight of Canandaigua Lake. It never failed to take their breath away.

"There it is!"

From their crested vantage, the girls could see the lake spread below them, all fifteen and a half miles of blue/green patchwork puddle. A few sailboats dotted the surface, struggling to find a breeze, while speedboats with water skiers in tow circled around them. *Like a cowboy throwing a lasso*, thought Yeardley. Along the shore, a ring of miniature white squares and the occasional circular trampoline float marked the swimming areas of individual cottages. One of them was Nola's. With Miami out of sight and out of mind, Lily could hardly wait to bask in the New York sun. Through her open window Shelby breathed deeply, the scent of honeysuckle welcoming her back. She felt lighter already.

"Ready?"

"Ready!!" Her sisters yelled in unison. Smiling broadly, Shelby put the car in gear, driving until the sound of crushed stone beneath the tires signaled their arrival at Nola's. They crunched down the tree-lined driveway, past the green lawn, freshly mowed, to the gateway that was a two-car garage. Shelby pulled into the open bay next to Nola's cherry red Camry and parked.

Set back from the lawn, Nola's vegetable garden was thriving. Rows of tomato plants hung heavy with green and red fruit like ornaments on a Christmas tree. Heads of lettuce tufted abundantly from the ground as well as peppers, cucumbers, onions, and chives. Nola's green thumb still had the magic touch.

Lily licked her lips, remembering the delicious salads that accompanied every dinner, and the homemade desserts. Dessert! That was one chore none of them had ever complained about; picking the juicy raspberries and plump blueberries for one of Nola's mouthwatering pastries or piling them fresh in a bowl with heavy cream drizzled over them. Lily was so disciplined with what she ate in Miami, but here, she could already feel herself losing control.

At this time of year, all the plants stood tall and full, their leaves creating a thick veil of green. Behind the garden, nearly obscured from view, stood the cottage. It was more of a house really, fully insulated and winterized with cedar shingles and green trim around the windows and doors. "Cottage" was an affectionate term from the throwback days when Shepardsville provided a summer escape for city residents from Memorial Day to Labor Day.

For as long as Nola could remember, the Hamilton family had always lived here. Her grandfather, Oscar, had built the cottage himself. Like most of the waterfront homes in the area, the house had two porches including one on the back or street-side that served as the main entrance. But the front porch was the pièce de résistance, overlooking the vast of expanse of lake just a stone's throw away.

Yeardley leaned across her sister to the steering wheel, and pressed firmly on the horn. "We're here!" Pumping out a few more honks, she was out of the car before Shelby or Lily had released their seat belts. "Aunt Nola, we're here!"

Bags in tow, the girls made their way to the cottage, holding up as Nola stepped onto the porch. Behind her, the screen door sprang back into place. Nola wore an apron, and a smudge of flour on her cheek that hid the fine lines of her welcoming smile. Her hair, auburn like Shelby's, gleamed red with silver streaks as she opened her arms wide for one of Nola's famous bear hugs. "My beautiful girls, you're here!"

"Aunt Nola!" Dropping their bags to the ground, all three flew into her arms, little girls once again.

"I've missed you!"

"You look fabulous!"

"What's that wonderful smell?"

41

Nola laughed, trying to make sense of all the chatter flying around her. "Hold on a minute, let me get a good look at you first."

One by one, she examined each of the girls closely framing their faces between her hands. "Shelby, my serious girl, it looks like we got you here just in time for a little R&R. Reading and rejuvenation." Nola's gray eyes twinkled. "Your mother said you've been working overtime on a big project at work, so I stocked the shelves in your room with some books I think you'll like. A little lake time should take care of everything else."

Nola turned her attention to Yeardley. "Now, Yeardley, what's this I hear about you making coffee at a financial company? That's what your mother said. Is 'barista' a real title?"

Yeardley looked happy enough, and healthy, fit from swimming every week. She had always been the athlete in the family. Even as a little girl, she had begged Nola to let her join the community baseball league. Then she had asked permission to turn the back lawn into a neighborhood whiffle ball field. When she was nine, she set her sights on water skiing. Nola had turned to her friends Bob and Becky Greene for help. Avid skiers themselves, it had taken them no time at all to teach Yeardley and their son Jackson how to glide across the water like pros.

"Barista." The word rolled off Nola's tongue. "It sounds very Yeardley, unconventional with a hint of tradition." With a knowing wink Nola shifted her gaze to Lily.

"Last but definitely not least, Princess Lily straight from the shores of Miami." Nola gave her another big hug. "We don't see nearly enough of you, you know?"

Lily flushed with guilt as Nola hurried to reassure her. "Don't feel bad, sweetheart. We just miss you, that's all. But you're here now, and that's all that matters." Nodding firmly, she wrapped an arm around Lily's shoulders, guiding her towards the door.

"Okay, troops, let's take it inside. You're all in your old rooms. There is plenty of time to check the place out, unpack, or keep me company in the kitchen while I finish putting dessert together. Your favorite," she said winking at her niece, "Lilyberry cobbler."

As if Nola had flipped a switch, the group chatter resumed, and the girls rushed inside, eager to see their old rooms. Lily reached hers first. At the top of the stairs, it was right next to Nola's. When she was little, this was important in case she fell out of bed or had a nightmare. At the first peep from next door, Nola had been at her side, ready to kiss any bumps or scare away any monsters. Lily's personal bodyguard. Diego filled that role now, keeping her close as they spooned in his black lacquer California king, one large arm wrapped securely around her waist. Still, the thought of Nola sleeping peacefully next door made Lily happy.

Down the hall from Lily, Shelby ran a finger across a row of books arranged tallest to shortest. Thirteen, fourteen, she counted silently. It would take more than a week to read all these.

Maybe she should stay longer. A giggle burst from her lips as she considered the possibility. How crazy would that be? And just as quickly she squelched the idea. She had already put in for five days vacation, and it looked like she might need a few more.

Pulling her phone from her bag, Shelby dialed her voicemail and listened yet again to a message delivered while her phone was in airplane mode. "Hi, Ms. Lane. This is Hillary Bark from Executive Recruiting Services in San Francisco. One of my platinum clients is very interested in meeting you. I can't name my client on the phone, but I'll give you a hint: they are a giant technology firm and number one on the West Coast. They are impressed by how flawlessly you guided your firm's newest product to market. Congratulations. Ms. Lane, if you share my client's interest, please call me back. I'll schedule a meeting right away and make all the necessary travel arrangements for you. Thank you."

Shelby saved the message again and checked the clock on her phone. It was 3:00 P.M. Matt was still at training. She was so excited to tell him about the call. It was killing her. Shelby sighed, placing her bag on the floral cushioned window seat that overlooked Nola's garden. She'd just have to keep herself busy until Matt got home. First, she would unpack. Then, if time allowed, she would sneak in a few chapters before dinner.

Throwing the window wide, Yeardley could not stop smiling at the sight of her beloved lake. She was back! She flopped on the bed, cradling her head in her hands, and stared at the pale yellow ceiling above her. How had she ever left? Everything about the place was special; the sunrises and sunsets, the sound of crackling bonfires at night, the fresh smell of morning after an evening rain storm, and the people, too. Nola, naturally, and Sheriff Merrill. He always carried candy in his pockets for the town kids, and biscuits for stray dogs. The Harpers who owned the local hardware store, and Miss Jean who ran the soda fountain at the pharmacy. The Greenes, of course. And Jackson. She closed her eyes, remembering her childhood sweetheart, but it hurt to think about him. It had been so many years since he had broken her heart.

"Shelby! Yeardley! Lily! Dinner!"

From the bottom of the stairs, Nola listened as three pairs of flip-flopped feet hurried to meet her. Tears sprang to her eyes, as she remembered footsteps past.

"Not now." She scolded herself, quickly brushing away her tears before the girls saw them. "When the time is right, I'll tell them."

Yeardley reached Nola first, breathless and flushed with excitement. "I can't believe we're here. The best place ever. Thank you so much for bringing us back." She hugged her aunt tightly.

Something smelled wonderful. Yeardley's stomach rumbled. "Hurry up, girls," she yelled to her sisters. "Last one to the table is a rotten egg!"

THE DINNER

Nola surveyed the dinner table, making sure nothing was missing or out of place. Made of solid oak, it had been in the family for generations, accommodating every kind of occasion from nightly family dinners to holiday gatherings and dinner parties. If she used the extra leaves stored in the hallway closet, it could seat up to ten people comfortably. But tonight, it was a simple square set just for the four of them. A centerpiece of brilliantly hued fresh cut flowers and white tapered candles added a special touch of elegance.

Satisfied that all was in order, Nola urged the girls to take their seats. "Don't be shy, start filling your plates. I've made plenty."

Nola passed a steaming platter of corn on the cob to Shelby. "Girls, do you remember how Shelby used to eat her corn neatly row by row?" she asked.

Shelby paused briefly, afraid all the butter would melt off her cob. "I'm not the only one who eats corn like that," she said, a little defensively. "I know other people who do too."

"You mean there are others?" Yeardley gasped in mock horror, and Lily laughed.

"Let me guess. Matt, right? You guys are two peas in a pod."

"Lily's right. You guys could be twins. It's sweet. Sickening, but sweet."

Nola shot Shelby an apologetic glance. "Sorry, I didn't mean to start anything."

"Don't be sorry. They would have found something to pick on eventually anyways. They're just jealous," Shelby said, pointedly extending a hand towards Yeardley. "May I have the potatoes, please?"

Handing her the bowl with narrowed eyes, Yeardley asked the obvious. "And what exactly am I jealous of again?" She planted both elbows firmly on the table sipping her wine and pretending to think.

Lily tried to help her out. "You've got to admit, Yeardley, Shelby does seem to have it all figured out. Great job. Great home. Great guy. You could learn something from her, you know?"

The whole table winced as Lily's words left them speechless. Mortified and embarrassed, she tried to apologize. "Yeardley, I am so sorry."

No one spoke. Lily played with the food on her plate, unable to meet her sister's rock hard glare. Those golden eyes sprinkled with bright copper flecks of color were one of Yeardley's best features, but right now, they blazed with anger.

Nola intervened, surprised how easily she slipped back into her role as peace keeper. "You know, even when you were little the three of you were nothing alike. Shelby was curious, but cautious. Yeardley was the daredevil, willing to try anything once. And Lily, you were always the little dreamer who liked to twirl and sing." Three pairs of eyes rested on her, questioning.

"My point is," she explained, "why should now be any different? What's important is that you're living the lives you want, lives of your own design."

"I'm sorry, Yeardley." Close to tears, Lily felt terrible. Nola was right. As usual.

"Apology accepted."

Though she was happy to see Lily smile again, Yeardley still felt the sting of her words. Because Lily wasn't completely wrong. Yeardley was a boat without an anchor, drifting aimlessly in search of the shore. She had her apartment, but it did not feel like home. She was employed, but not inspired. Her friends were great, but they were becoming increasingly unavailable. Every weekend, it seemed, she was going to a wedding, ushering one more single friend into the married couples club. The truth was, she envied her sisters and what they had.

But thinking about it wasn't going to make it better. "Hey, I thought we were here to celebrate Aunt Nola's birthday," she said, changing the subject. "So how are we going to do that? Shelby, what do you think?"

Shelby dabbed a napkin to the corners of her mouth, chewing slowly and savoring every last bite of her dinner. Why did food always taste better when someone else cooked it; especially when that someone was Nola? Smiling appreciatively at the cook, she said, "That was delicious, Aunt Nola, thank you."

Yeardley and Lily were waiting on her, patiently, expectantly. She was the oldest, the leader, and she always had a plan. Shelby flushed. In her haste to get here, she hadn't even thought about Nola's birthday, at least, not in the planning sense. She had really dropped the ball this time.

Clearing her throat, Shelby shifted self-consciously in her chair, tucking her hair behind one ear. "The plan," she began, "is to make this the best birthday celebration ever. But first we have to find out what would make Aunt Nola happy."

Yeardley and Lily nodded their agreement, turning in tandem to Nola. "Okay, Aunt Nola, what's your birthday wish?"

"I already got it," Nola smiled, raising her glass to the girls. "I wished you girls could come visit, and here you are, just like old times." Her eyes looked like glassy pools in the candlelight.

"Don't cry, Aunt Nola."

"Yeah, this is supposed to be a happy time," Yeardley reminded her. "It's your time, so no crying allowed, not even happy tears."

"I'm so happy you're all here, you've no idea, but no promises on the tears," Nola chuckled. "We can have a small party, just the four of us."

"That's it!" cried Lily.

"That's what?"

"We'll throw Aunt Nola a birthday bash, with food and decorations, and music, and we'll invite all of her friends, and Mom and Dad too."

Lily had a knack for the spectacular, and her excitement was infectious.

"It'll be huge," added Yeardley thinking of all the people they would have to invite. "Definitely an outdoor party."

Shelby agreed. "Something this big requires a lot of thought and planning. We don't want to forget anything, or overlook anyone."

Nola cleared her throat. "I think you already have. What about what I think? I'm not sure this is such a good idea."

"What? Why not?" The party planners shrieked in disbelief.

"Well, for one thing, I'm not a fan of the spotlight, all those people. And for another, why would anyone even want to come?"

"You really don't know, do you?" Shelby asked, after a moment's pause. Squeezing her aunt's hand she gestured to her sisters. "Nola Ann Hamilton, you welcomed us into your home and created a heaven on earth for three little girls. For sixty-five years, you have given your heart and soul to your community, your neighbors, and friends. You are incredibly special to so many people. This party is a chance for all of us to say 'We love you Nola.' "

Nola made no attempt to hide the tears streaming down her face. Her heart was near to bursting. "Thank you." Her voice cracked as sobs threatened to take over. "I couldn't love you girls any more if I tried."

Glancing around the table, Yeardley was surrounded by crying women. "I thought we said no crying allowed," she protested, tears starting to rain down her own cheeks. "Oh, hell! We'll never get through the week if we keep this up."

LILY

When dinner was finished, we divided up the party planning responsibilities. Shelby was in charge of Nola's party. She handed out our assignments judiciously, and according to our strengths.

Yeardley, through years of playing community sports, and socializing in general, was most connected to the people of Shepardsville. After making a convincing case to Shelby, she was charged with inviting all of Nola's friends and neighbors to the party.

"We have to work quickly," Shelby stated firmly. "We don't have time for printed invitations."

"Don't worry," Yeardley assured her. "I'll invite everyone personally. It means a lot of driving around and a lot of talking, but it'll be fun to see everyone again."

Shelby nodded, checking 'invitations' off her to-do list. "Lily, I think your assignment is pretty obvious."

My job was to create the most fabulous production the lake had seen in years. From concept to finish, Nola's party would be entirely of my own design. I could hardly wait to get started. This party was exactly what I needed to sink my teeth into; a project that said 'Lily Lane was here.' Lisa and the others back at the office would not have the opportunity to roll their eyes and insinuate that I was resting on Diego's laurels.

I wandered into the living room, homey and rustic with rough-hewn walls, and comfortably worn furniture, and a wall of windows overlooking the lake. In one corner was a television, but everyone knew it was only called to action as a last resort. Indoor time was for games and such.

On rainy days, we could spend hours putting puzzles together on the old, chipped side table. We learned to play cards. Round after round of Go Fish and Crazy Eights, until we clamored for something else. Reaching into the toy chest, Nola would pull out our favorite board games: Uncle Wiggly, Mall Madness, and Twister. My own obsession was sitting at the miniature craft table Nola had purchased especially for us. A small square table with four kid-size chairs, it was just right for my budding artistic talents. Feeling like a real artist, I would spread my paints out in front of me, eager to put my brush to paper.

The lake was my favorite subject. Sometimes, I would try to capture it waking up, the early morning light casting a rosy hue upon its surface. Other times, I concentrated on the perfect sunset sinking into the water and dipping below the horizon. At the end of each summer, Aunt Nola would pick one of my paintings to frame, and hang it on the living room wall.

53

The lights in the living room were already on as I made my way into the room, settling into one of the cozy, overstuffed chairs. On the wall across from me were the paintings, ten in all. The oldest ones were little more than water colored swirls of blues, yellows, and oranges. The last painting, done when I was a teenager, showed much more promise. It was a sunset over the lake. In the foreground, Aunt Nola's boat floated quietly at the dock, one of many that fringed the shoreline.

So, what will make this party the talk of the summer? I wondered, staring at the bookcase next to my chair. Large books and small, thin and fat, Aunt Nola always kept the shelves well-stocked like a true librarian. Casually, I perused the multi-colored spines. The answer had to be here somewhere.

It was. *The Social History of Lake Canandaigua*, was exactly what I needed. It was a large book, heavy with lots of black and white pictures from summers past. Images of boats, golf, an occasional wedding and lots and lots of tennis jumped off the pages. Family after family enjoying all that summer at the lake had to offer. I flipped through the pages, hungry for ideas.

I was almost halfway through the book before I found it, a summertime tradition dating back to the 1920s. Summer's-end parties were a kind of 'last hurrah' for seasonal residents, before returning home to school and work. The parties were so popular, they were held in a local barn, the only space large enough to accommodate the expansive crowd. Food, dancing, costumes and fireworks were the staples of every summer's-end party, but each featured its own unique theme: Masquerade Ball, Neptune's Ball, Shipwreck, and Hunter's Ball, to name a few.

My mind started to race. Of course! We would throw a themed party that evoked the nostalgic feeling of the old days. A "Retro Chic Lake Party" complete with summer foods, elegant decorations, fireworks, music; it would be an old fashioned picnic with class. Traditional but elegant, just like Nola. Thrilled, I jumped from my chair, and rushed to tell Shelby.

SHELBY

The dinner dishes were washed, dried, and put away. I glanced around the kitchen making sure everything was in its proper place. Nola wouldn't mind, but I hated it when people put my things away improperly.

"Shelby," Lily stormed into the kitchen. "I have it all figured out. We're going to have a Retro Chic Lake-themed birthday party for Aunt Nola!" Waving her arms and gesturing towards the lake, Lily was clearly excited.

"Huh?" I asked, clueless. What in the world was retro chic lake?

"Retro Chic Lake!" Lily repeated, with a greater sense of urgency.

"Yeah. I heard you," I told her. "I just don't know what that means, Lily."

Lily rolled her eyes at me, and placed a large book on the kitchen counter. "Come look at this."

She thumbed through the book, finally settling on several pages filled with pictures. Ladies from bygone decades smiled at me in their chic summer dresses and hats. Men in pressed khakis and short-sleeved dress shirts gathered in tight circles telling stories, some with cigars and drinks in their hand. Campfires glowed beneath cooking grates laden with grilled food, while linen-draped tables stood by, waiting patiently for diners to vacate the dance floor.

Lily was right. There was a chicness to the pictures. "Where is this?" I asked, genuinely curious.

"Right here on Canandaigua! I found this book in the living room. They used to have end-of-the-summer parties. Each year was a different theme, and everyone who was anyone was there. Look how proper everything looks. You don't see that anymore, Shelby. So I decided the party itself will be the theme. We'll make it a tribute to days gone by. I'll decorate the entire yard with inspiration from these pictures. We'll get a big white tent, round tables, white tablecloths, lots of fresh summer flowers, a band and..." Lily took a quick breath, and I took the opportunity to bring her back to earth.

"Wait a minute, Princess Lily." I raised my hand, urging her to slow down. "It sounds perfect. It really does! But we only have a week to pull this party together. And if Yeardley strikes out inviting people, we won't have any party at all. So how do you propose we get all that stuff here by next Saturday? This isn't Miami, you know. We don't have endless resources here."

"Shelby, you are not dealing with an amateur. This is what I do! I will pull it all together, and mark my words, it will be the talk of the lake." Gently, she forced my hand back to my side. "Now, I'm going to go make a list of all the things we need. And, first thing tomorrow, we'll get started. Capice?"

"Whatever you say, Lily. But I'm telling you right now, you better have a 'Plan B.' We just need this to be special for Aunt Nola. It doesn't have to be the event of the season."

"Oh, it will be, Shelby! After all, it's a Lily Lane design." She smiled as she snapped her fingers.

I rolled my eyes, but Lily was gone, in search of paper for her lists.

I could feel the tension rising in the back of my neck. I wished I could share Lily's enthusiasm, but all I saw was a monumental amount of work to be done in one short week. So much for Nola's R&R. This was going to be a working vacation.

Reaching for my phone, I called Matt. He picked up on the first ring.

"Hi, Babe. How's it going? You made it to Nola's safely?"

"Hi, yourself, and yes, we all made it here safe and sound though I might have to murder Lily soon."

"You're kidding, I hope." Matt's laugh made me smile, too.

"Of course I am. We've decided to throw a birthday party for Nola. Not a big deal really. But you know Lily. She doesn't do anything small. So now we have one week to pull together a world-class extravaganza."

"Well, if anyone can pull it off, it's you and your sisters."

"So if they're helping me with the party, then maybe you can help me figure out something else."

"What's that?"

I was so excited, I nearly shouted, "Guess who got a call from Executive Recruiting Services of San Francisco?" I cut him off before he could guess. "Me!"

"Can you believe it, honey? Amber Sky Technologies wants to meet with me. At least I think it's Amber Sky. The recruiter wouldn't say for sure, but I'm almost positive that's who it is."

I took a breath giving Matt a chance to speak. "Baby, I'm so proud of you. I told you your work on OAR wouldn't go unnoticed."

"Yeah, but I didn't think it would be Amber Sky Technologies that noticed me. I can't believe it. This is amazing."

"You're amazing," Matt said warmly.

I wished we were together so I could hug him close. "The job's not mine yet. But you know how these things work. They wouldn't have even contacted me if they didn't consider me qualified, or if they weren't truly interested in me."

"True."

Lily entered the kitchen, waving papers in her hand. "Matt, I have to go. Princess Lily's on a party rampage and I have to go rein her in. I'll call you tomorrow. We can talk more then. Love you."

I hung up the phone and braced myself for Lily's onslaught.

"I have the whole thing worked out, Shelby. We'll use New York Rentals for the tent, tables, and chairs. Just let them know how many we need and when. I'll go see Mrs. Rollins tomorrow. She always had the most amazing flower gardens. Maybe she'll help us out with floral arrangements for the tables. Nola wouldn't want anyone but Greene's Market catering the event. You should call them tomorrow, too. Becky can help you with the menu."

Lily pulled a sheet of paper from her stack of notes. "Now, here's a list of all the supplies we need. I'm not sure where to get the fireworks, but you'll figure it out. Also, you need to look into the entertainment. I'd love a live band that plays the oldies, but I'll settle for a D.J."

Lily pushed the stack of papers into my hand. "If you have any questions, make sure you ask me so we're on the same page. I have a vision of how everything needs to look, and I want it to be perfect. Oh, one last thing. Do you need the car tomorrow? I want to head over to Shepardsville and check out stores there. We need a boat load of decorations and party favors for all of the guests."

Not bothering to wait for my reply, Lily sailed out of the kitchen once again. "Good night, Shelby. You should get to bed, too. We have a busy day tomorrow."

If I hadn't seen it with my own eyes, I would never have believed the perky dictator in pink was my very own baby sister. Impressive. But I wasn't stupid. Lily might be leading the way, but I knew I would be handling the details. While Lily focused on the most creative aspects of our 'project,' I would stand guard over important things like budget, scope, and schedule. Looking over the scrawling cursive of Lily's notes, I felt the tension ascending rapidly from my neck to my head. If we pulled this off, it would be a miracle.

SUNDAY

YEARDLEY

I cranked the radio and opened the sunroof, letting the wind blow through the car like a fan. Settling deeper into the comfy leather seat, I wished I could stay like this forever. There was nothing better than driving around on a beautiful day, not a care in the world except which junk food craving to satisfy first. God bless Nola. She had refused to let me leave the house without a travel mug of fresh squeezed lemonade, homemade chocolate chip cookies, and a bag of salt and vinegar potato chips for good measure. "Something to tide you over until dinner."

And it was a good thing too. I had totally skipped lunch, trying to get away from Shelby, her marching orders still ringing in my ears.

"Now, don't forget to invite the Carpenters, and the Crockers, and the Millers," she reminded me, furiously jotting notes in her party planner. "Oh, and don't forget the Edwards!"

Shelby sat in her makeshift office, formerly the dining room table. An open laptop rested nearby, fringed with colored sticky notes, but Shelby ignored it. Instead, she was scrutinizing the contents of the papers in her hand. A single index finger danced back and forth across the page as she carefully read every word. Nothing would get by her.

"Shelby," I said as she scribbled madly, blind and deaf to anything besides her work. "Shelby!" I grabbed her wrist, and forced her to look at me. "Shelby, we went over this already, you, me, and Lily. I've got this. I'll get everybody here. Don't worry."

"This party has to be perfect."

Of course it did. I tried to remember if Shelby had always been so uptight. Not always. During our summers at the lake, Mom's mini-me would miraculously disappear, and for a few weeks, Shelby was just my sister. We played pirates in the cove as kids. As teenagers, we drenched our bodies in baby oil and baked in the sun, listening to music and talking about boys. It was time for *that* Shelby to make an appearance again.

"It's going to be perfect," I promised. "With the Lane Girls on the job, what else could it be?"

Shelby smiled, not entirely convinced.

"Seriously, Shel, I know you think I'm crazy, but I'm not an idiot. I won't let you or Nola down."

Shelby's face softened. She looked younger, more carefree. "You're right. It's going to be a great party, one for the ages. But you better get to it if we're going to have anyone here at all. Remember, the Carpenters, the Crockers, and the Millers."

She opened her mouth to speak again, but I beat her to the punch, "I know. I know. I won't forget the Edwards."

Grabbing my snacks and drink from Nola, I escaped through the kitchen and raced to the garage where Shelby's voice couldn't follow me. I knew what I was doing, and sooner or later she would realize it too.

I had volunteered for the job knowing that Shelby and Lily were struggling to find a task for me, something even I couldn't screw up.

"How about set up?" Lily suggested, ruling it out before I could even speak. "On second thought, that falls under theme and design. I've got that under control."

"We need a menu," offered Shelby. "And estimated quantities so we don't run out of food. And a budget. And someone to oversee all the costs and expenses." Shelby's list was growing longer, but she wasn't asking for help.

"Why don't I handle the invitations?" I said, choosing to ignore their worried glances. "I mean, Lily's got the whole set up thing down, and Shelby, it sounds like you've got everything else under control. The only things missing from this party are the guests. So I'll take care of that."

"She does know a lot of Nola's friends," Lily spoke out loud, but deferred to our older sister. "What do you think, Shelby?"

"Hello, standing right here! Would you please stop talking about me like I'm not even in the room, and stop looking at me like I'm some kind of incompetent moron. I'm a big girl. I can handle inviting a few people to a party. Besides, chatting up people is what I do best."

I had them there, and they knew it. Both of my sisters had years of experience dragging me away from conversations; with my friends, coaches, sales clerks, the mailman, pretty much anyone I came into contact with.

"Come on, Yeardley, we're leaving now. C'mon, Yeardley, I want to go. Come on, Yeardley, it's time go home." Finally, being a 'people person' was paying off.

My first stop was the Crockers. Mrs. Crocker is my mom's age. They were best friends all through school and college. When Mom and Dad got married, Mrs. Crocker was a bridesmaid.

"It was such a beautiful wedding," Mrs. Crocker would say in a dreamy voice, "and your father, the young professor, he was so handsome. All of us girls were a little bit in love with him, you know."

Mr. Crocker must have loved hearing that, but he was a good sport. If it bothered him, he never let on. "Yes, dear, we've heard the story before, but I don't think that's why Yeardley is here."

I've known the Crockers since our first summer at the lake. Too young to be left alone, Nola would take us to work with her at the library where she was the Assistant Director. Mr. Crocker was the Director, but he was well aware that "your aunt is the real boss around here." They made a great team, creating a special place for the local community and their adopted summer residents to enjoy.

Shelby loved going to the library and reading for hours on end. Lily was content to color and draw, or play dress up in the Theater Corner. But I was bored. Spotting a small playground just outside, I begged Nola to let me go. "Please? I promise I won't leave the playground. Please?"

Mr. Crocker even took up my cause. "Come on now, Nola, let the girl go. You can keep an eye on her from your window. She'll be fine."

Nola nodded uncertainly, not yet convinced, and I dashed out the door before she could change her mind. "Be careful," she called. "Don't talk to strangers!"

Only one other kid was at the playground when I got there, a girl named Ruth. "Have you ever touched the sky?" she asked from her perch on a swing.

"Plenty of times," I snorted, sizing up her friend potential.

"Bet I can touch it first."

"Not if you just sit there, you won't." Jumping on the swing beside her, I pumped my legs as fast as I could, pushing it higher and higher until we actually touched the sky. We flew for a long time, back and forth, until we were dizzy and tired.

I looked around for something else to do. Spotting an old tennis ball, I tossed it to Ruth. She caught it with ease, and fired it back hard.

"Let's play catch." Red haired and freckled, Ruth looked like Raggedy Ann, but she played ball like Derek Jeter.

We played catch for a while, silently challenging and pushing, stretching out the distance between us until we fell into an easy rhythm of give and take.

"You're pretty good," she said, throwing another rocket my way. "Do you play at home?"

"Sometimes," I answered, surprised how much Shepardsville already felt like home. "In gym, mostly. How about you?"

"Oh yeah. Shepardsville has a great summer league. I'm in the minors right now, but when I'm ten, I'll play in the majors. You should come watch sometime. We practice during the week and have games on the weekends."

From that moment on, and every summer after, Ruth Donovan was my best friend in Shepardsville. Ruth had lived there her whole life with her parents and little brother Davey, a red headed leprechaun full of sweetness and mischief like his sister. Her dad Dave was a bank manager who moonlighted as coach of the high school basketball team during the school year. In the summer, he managed Donovan's Devils little league team. Ruth introduced me to him after practice one day. "Dad, this is my friend, Yeardley."

Towering over me like a giant California redwood, Mr. Donovan crouched down, bringing his green eyes level with mine, and shook my hand.

69

"How do you do, Yeardley? You're Nola Hamilton's niece, aren't you?" I nodded as he continued. "She's a wonderful woman. We all love her around here. I bet you're a lot like her." Mr. Donovan had a way of making people feel special.

"Mr. Donovan," I blurted his name, hoping his fondness for Nola would carry over to me. "Do you think I could join your team? Can I be one of Donovan's Devils?"

He tilted his head to one side, sizing me up. "Well, you're just a little bit of a thing, aren't you?" He crossed his arms, rubbing his chin and thinking out loud, "Though I suppose if you're anything like your aunt, you've got a heart that doesn't quit. And Ruth tells me you've got a killer arm."

I waited for him to decide, the suspense killing me. I had never wanted anything more in my life.

Mr. Donovan stood and spoke to Ruth. "We better get going or we'll be late for dinner. Mom will not be happy."

He looked at me, his face serious. "Practices are at 4 o'clock Monday, Wednesday, and Friday. Games on the weekends. You'll need a glove, I'll take care of the rest."

Taking Ruth's hand, he started to walk away, then stopped, as if he had forgotten something. With a twist, he turned and smiled. "Welcome to the team, Yeardley."

The Donovans still lived in the house Ruth had grown up in. It was a two-story log cabin framed by yellow rose bushes, a nod to Mrs. Donovan's Texas roots, and a small vineyard in the back, for Mr. Donovan's experimental wine making. They were on the front porch when I arrived, soaking up the afternoon sun from a pair of high-back Adirondack chairs.

Mr. Donovan stood at the top of the steps rubbing his eyes in disbelief. "Honey, look, it's Yeardley Lane, my number one third baseman." Pulling me into a bear hug, he growled affectionately. "Where have you been, girl?"

Grinning like a fool, I stepped back to greet them both. "Hey, Coach. Hi, Mrs. Donovan. Can Ruth come out and play?" Who said 'you can't go home again'?

The time flew as we reminisced about the good old days, and caught up on the present. I had not seen or talked to Ruth in forever. She was a married mother of two now, teaching fifth grade, and living just outside of Albany.

"She'll definitely want to come home for this. You don't mind if we tell her, do you?" Mrs. Donovan asked, when I told her about the party.

"Of course not. I'd love to see Ruth. Nola would too. Tell her the party won't be complete without her."

I glanced at my watch. The day was disappearing, and I still had a slew of stops to make before my job was done. Time to pick up the pace and pump up the volume. I smiled brightly at Ruth's parents; they knew everybody in town.

"Can I ask you guys a favor?"

A short time later, I was back on the road making a beeline for downtown Shepardsville, confident the Donovans' had my back.

"Don't worry, Yeardley. You take care of the folks in town, and we'll tell everybody else. We'll call, we'll email, hell, we'll send smoke signals if we have to. It's a party for Nola after all."

My eyes misted. I shoved my sunglasses over them, so they couldn't see. Clearly my sisters and I weren't the only ones devoted to Nola. Giving the Donovans each a hug, I thanked them again and rushed to my car, before I made a sappy fool of myself.

I can't prove it, but I swear Walt Disney had a hand in creating Shepardsville. With its charming oak lined streets, purple painted fire hydrants, spinning barber shop pole, and elaborate wood carvings of animals gracing front lawns and storefronts, it practically screams Magic Kingdom. Maybe Mr. Bluebird wasn't sitting on my shoulder, but I was one happy girl pulling up to Murphy's Old Thyme Pharmacy.

I entered the store, pausing to take in the quiet bustle of customers browsing the aisles, exchanging greetings with pieces of gossip.

"Did you hear someone 'borrowed' Ted Mason's boat last night? Woke up to his dog barking and when he went to investigate, there it was unmoored, empty beer cans floating all around it."

"That's awful. I bet it was teenagers. They're getting more and more out of hand every year."

"Dumber is more like it," I thought, recalling the pranks my friends and I had pulled over the years. Harmless stunts mostly, but still, I'm pretty sure we never left any damning evidence behind.

"Well, look who the cat dragged in." A deep voice boomed behind me. I jumped out of my skin.

"Hi, Mr. Murphy. How are you?"

The town pharmacist had to be pushing seventy, but you would never know it to look at him. His salt and pepper hair, combed to one side, was still more dark than light. The boyish dimples on his wrinkle-free cheeks gave him a youthful appearance. He was a big man, well padded with an oversized belly. He reminded me of a giant teddy bear in a white pharmacy coat.

"Just fine, thanks for asking. But what about you? How long's it been? Are your sisters with you?" He craned his neck, searching for Shelby and Lily.

"Not right now, but we're all here visiting Nola," I explained. "You know it's her birthday. We're throwing a party to celebrate. I hope you'll come."

"Wouldn't miss it. I love a good party. Will there be dancing?" Mr. Murphy shuffled his feet in what I assumed were some kind of dance steps. "Nola and I went to prom together, you know? We really knew how to cut a rug."

Stifling a giggle, I prayed Lily had made appropriate musical arrangements for the event. I could not see Nola or Mr. Murphy, or any of their friends for that matter, grinding or twerking the night away.

"Count on it," I assured him, waving as I moved towards the back of the store. "I've got to invite Miss Jean now. I'll see you later, Mr. Murphy."

As expected, I found Miss Jean at the soda fountain, whipping up a variety of frozen treats. A group of hungry kids waited impatiently, swiveling themselves to distraction on the red and chrome stools that lined the counter. Putting a finger to my lips, I motioned for them to stay quiet. Slipping behind the counter, I placed my hands over Miss Jean's eyes.

"Guess who?"

Without missing a beat, Miss Jean put the finishing touches on a deluxe banana split, a final squirt of whip cream with a spoonful of cherries on top.

"I suppose you'll be wanting your usual? Chocolate malt, extra thick."

The kids shrieked in delight. I couldn't help laughing as we hugged hello.

"How did you know it was me? That's amazing!"

"Oh, Yeardley," she said touching a hand to my cheek, "you're a hard person to forget."

She put her hands on my shoulders, turning me to face her young customers. "Kids, meet my friend, Yeardley. She's been coming to my ice cream counter since she was your age. See, that's her in the picture up there."

Seven pairs of eyes looked to the wall where a 5x7 hung from a rusty nail. It was a picture of me and Ruth. We were sitting in front of a mountain of ice cream, spoons at the ready.

God, I remember that day. You bet that we couldn't eat the Mt. Everest Sundae in fifteen minutes."

"If you did, you'd get free ice cream for the rest of the summer."

"And if we didn't, we'd get one heck of a stomach ache."

"What happened?" A chorus of voices chirped.

"We ate the whole sundae, of course. Then we had the worst stomachaches of our lives. Let that be a lesson," I warned. "There is such a thing as too much ice cream."

Miss Jean served up the last of the orders, turning her full attention on me. "I was just tired of making the two of you malteds every single day. Thought I could cure your cravings for a while."

"That you did. You pissed off Nola pretty good, too. I remember her saying she didn't know who was worse, me for eating the sundae or you for putting me up to it."

"Achh, no harm, no foul. You survived, and Nola forgave me a long time ago. Now she's the one stopping by to bother me for ice cream."

"I didn't know she had such a sweet tooth."

I pictured Nola and Miss Jean hanging out together at the soda fountain, talking over some frozen concoction of Miss Jean's making. The girls having fun.

"You have to come by the house, Miss Jean. We're throwing a party for Nola's birthday. I know it would mean the world to her to have you there."

"You don't have to ask me twice. Would it be all right if I made a special ice cream cake for the occasion? I know all of Nola's favorite flavors."

For the next half hour, I sipped on a chocolate malt, helping Miss Jean decide which flavor combination to use for Nola's cake: strawberry/banana/peach, chocolate/cookie dough/Dulce de Leche, or black raspberry/chocolate chip/raspberry swirl. A sudden flashback of Mt. Everest made me queasy.

"Sorry, Miss Jean, I've got to run," I apologized. "More invitations to give out."

Elbow deep in ideas, she barely noticed me leaving. "Okay, Yeardley. I'll see you at the party."

Several hours later, the sun was sitting low in the sky, signaling me back to the cottage for cocktail hour. I had spent the entire afternoon running in and out of shops, inviting all of Nola's friends to the party; the Schroeders and the Johnsons, the Todds and the Petersons, the Williams and the Martins, and of course the Edwards. They would all be there. And more. Nola was going to be blown away when everyone showed up. I was ready to prop up my feet and enjoy a nice glass of wine. I just had one more stop to make.

Greene's Market stands exactly on the town line. It is the unofficial welcome center of Shepardsville. A combination general store, produce stand, and bakery, it was founded in the late 1800s by the impressively tall William Greene, privately referred to by his customers as the Greene Giant. Despite his intimidating size and anti-social tendencies, William's market was special. It was the origin of one-stop-shopping, where a person could get milk and feed for the chickens and catch up on the news of the day all in one place. It was the town hub.

After William died, his eldest son Bart took over the operations. He added some new touches including a service station and an open air produce market that operates spring through fall. Bart and his wife Mary had four children, three girls and a boy named Robert, Bob for short.

Bob inherited the market when his parents retired, his sisters having moved away to raise families of their own. Bob and his wife Becky did the Greene name proud with their hard working ways and creative sensibilities. After Becky won the annual Shepardsville Grape Festival pie contest five years in a row, they decided to expand the Market again. Soon, there was a new in-house bakery offering fresh breads and baked goods, and of course pies of every kind.

Shelby, Lily, and I each had our favorite pie from Greene's Market. Mine was raspberry, Shelby loved the apple caramel walnut, and Lily could eat a whole chocolate chip pie by herself. Every Sunday morning, Nola would take us to Greene's to get eggs and milk for the week; and every week, one of us got to pick out a pie for Sunday dinner. So routine were our visits, Bob swore he could tell time by them.

"Better hurry up and stock the pie table, Becky. Nola and The Pie Sisters are here to pick up their dessert."

Nola and the Greenes went way back. "I can't remember a time I didn't know Becky or Bob," Nola had told her once. "Becky's been one of my closest friends since grade school. Bob and I worked together at the Market when we were in high school."

I loved Greene's Market; the smells of fresh fruit and baked goods, horns honking in the parking lot as customers came and went, shouting a friendly hello. And the laughter. There was always a lot of laughter at Greene's.

I entered through the green house nursery, an organized grid of plants, herbs and flowers. I used to help out here sometimes, when the Greene's were short handed. I did whatever they needed, but usually, it was working in the green house, keeping the plants watered and cool from the hot sun that beat through the glass roof above. As customers loaded their carts from the make-shift wooden pallet tables, I would run to the back for more, restocking the black and green plastic containers as fast as they were taken away.

Jackson and I had made a game of it, taking different routes to the back each time. Dodging and weaving our way through the aisles, we raced the clock to see who was fastest. Just a little competitive. For old time's sake, I doubled-timed it into the store.

Inside, my racing feet stopped short at the sight of Bob and Becky's only son standing a stone's throw away from me. Jackson stood in the middle of command central, a large square counter equipped with four registers and a coffee station offering a hot cup of joe for a quarter.

He was even taller than I remembered. His youthful, gangly frame was now the lean, muscular body of a twenty-eight year old man. Standing with his hands on his hips, he looked like a pirate scanning the ocean for signs of trouble. Soft waves of sandy blonde hair streaked gold by the sun fell across his tanned brow. Mindlessly, he brushed it away, revealing a pair of gorgeous green eyes beneath.

I watched as Jackson chatted with one of the cashiers. She was a pretty young girl with long dark hair like a satin curtain. She tossed it flirtatiously, from side to side as she spoke to him.

Jackson laughed, gently removing her hand that had somehow landed on his bicep.

Hussy. I heard the air hissing through my gritted teeth.

"Yeardley, is that you?"

I had been spotted.

"Becky! How are you?" We met just shy of the checkout counter, and hugged.

"I'm so happy to see you. You look great!" I took a step back, admiring the woman who had shared her blonde good looks with her son. "You really do."

"Don't be silly. I'm an old woman. But you," it was her turn to check me out, "you most definitely are not. You're gorgeous, Yeardley. And all grown up."

Still holding me at arm's length, she yelled over to her son, "Jackson, look who's here. It's Yeardley! Come say hello."

My heart pounded as he walked casually around the counter to join us. I struggled to keep my breathing even. Wearing a baby blue t-shirt and jeans that hugged in all the right places, he looked hot. I stuck out my hand, hoping it wasn't sweaty. His cool gaze washed over me, sending a shiver of excitement down my spine.

"Isn't she beautiful, Jackson? Oh, honey, we've missed you around here. A handshake, really? We're family. Jackson give the girl a hug."

Becky chatted away, oblivious of my nerves. Jackson shrugged, a goofy smile lighting up his handsome face. He opened his arms to me.

"Mother knows best."

I laughed, stepping into his embrace. It was familiar, safe, and wonderful.

"Hey, beautiful," he whispered against my ear, or did I imagine that?

We separated, smiling awkwardly as the moment of togetherness passed. My nerves threatened to take over again. Time to go. Focusing all of my attention on Becky, I invited the Greenes to Nola's party.

"Just bring yourselves. We're under strict orders from Nola, no gifts."

"That sounds like her," Becky agreed. "But let us know if there's anything else we can do to help. What about food?"

"I'm surprised you haven't heard from Shelby. She probably wanted me to invite you before she contacted you about catering. I'll let her know when I get home." I reached to give Becky another quick hug good-bye.

"It was so great to see you, Becky. You too." I dared to look in Jackson's direction.

He had not moved the entire time his mom and I were talking, staring at me as if I had two heads. My cheeks flamed. I needed a pre-dinner swim to bring my temperature back to normal.

"Okay. I'll see you in a few days." I walked to my car resisting the urge to run. I was dying to get away as fast as I could.

"Yeardley! Wait!" Jackson approached the car, a flat white box in his hand. "Welcome back."

He handed me the box through the window. A clear plastic square on top revealed a golden brown crust inside with a starburst of red in the middle. It was a raspberry pie.

"Your favorite. Right?"

He remembered.

"Yes," I said, shoving my sunglasses over my eyes once again. "Thank you, Jackson."

I started the car and waved good-bye, keeping my eyes on the road ahead of me until he was nothing more than a speck in my rearview mirror.

Yeardley found me where she had left me. At the dining room table, buried in piles of papers and notes. She poked her head through the kitchen doorway.

"Holy Jesus!" Yeardley let out a low whistle.

"Yeah, I know." I nodded slowly, "This party's becoming bigger than the Presidential Inauguration. I have stacks of notes for every party service from here to New York City. If Lily texts me one more thing to do, I'm going to change my phone number."

Sinking into the chair beside me, Yeardley looked at me sympathetically.

I shuffled a few of the papers in front of me.

"I have confirmation on most of the details for the party. I talked to a fireworks technician. His name is Cam Brown. I've hired him to manage the fireworks display. We have a DJ, too. Carson Andrews. He's the grandson of Nola's friend, Mrs. Andrews, from the Garden Club. I explained to him what Lily wants for music, and he didn't run. So that's good. We need to feed these guys, though, so be sure you add them to the invitation head count."

Yeardley nodded. "Do you have a pencil? I'll add them to the list."

I handed her a pencil. "How did you make out today?"

"Well, I don't think we have to worry about not having guests for the party. Pretty much the whole town seems to be coming."

Holy crap! How were we ever going to pull this off?

"Shelby? Hey, Shelby!" Yeardley waved her hand in front of my face. "Are you okay? You look like you've seen a ghost."

"I'm fine. But tell me something." I looked at Yeardley. "What if this party is a total bomb?"

"You mean in a good way, right?" Yeardley joked. "Of course it's going to be Da Bomb. Lily wouldn't have it any other way."

She was right, of course. "Except Lily's not here. Yeardley, you have no idea how much I still have to do."

Yeardley looked at me strangely. "Who are you and what have you done with my super woman sister, Shelby?"

"I'm not Super Woman," I snorted derisively.

"Pretty darn close," Yeardley countered. "You're the one who always gets things done."

"Well, somebody has to," I argued.

"That's true," Yeardley agreed. "But only because you don't ever give anyone else a chance to step up to the plate. How do you know someone else won't take care of things if you never let them?"

I opened my mouth and shut it again. What could I say to that? Through the window, I could see the sun slowly making its descent. I always thought this was the most enchanting time of day at the lake. When we were little and the sun began to set, it was a signal for us all to meet in the living room. Aunt Nola would go to the bookshelves and get the magic candle. She would place it on the coffee table and my sisters and I would all hold hands in a circle.

"Ready?" Aunt Nola would ask each of us.

"Ready!" we'd cry.

"Okay, girls. Let's do it," she'd say. With tiny voices, we would warble our magic candle song. "I love you.... today and everyday.... I love you." When the nonsensical song was over we would squeeze each other's hands as tightly as we could. It was a connection that said our family bond was unbreakable.

Afterwards, Nola would blow out the candle and shoo us upstairs. "Time for bed, girls. Everyone in their pajamas." We never went willingly. We did not want the day to end. But Nola would promise: the sooner we went to bed the sooner morning would come.

All these years later, it was still a priority. The first thing I did when we arrived at the lake was to scan the living room for the magical candle, sitting on the shelf, where it always was. It represented family and unconditional love. A smile formed on my lips.

"What's so funny?" Yeardley asked.

"Not funny. I'm smiling because I was just remembering the magic candle. Do you remember the song?"

"Of course!" Yeardley smiled, too. "I would never forget that song."

We sat quietly for a moment with our memories. I loved my sisters. Even when they were irritatingly annoying, I hated to see them sad or unhappy. I would do anything for them. But maybe I needed to back off a little. Maybe, I needed to ask them for help once in a while.

"Yeardley?"

"Hmm?" With chin in hand, Yeardley was still daydreaming.

"I need your help."

Yeardley snapped to attention. "Really? Seriously? You trust me to help you?"

She looked stunned but thrilled. I felt awful. Yeardley could do anything she set her mind to. You just had to let her try.

"Would you take over the catering?"

Yeardley's eyes grew dark. She blinked and they were light again. "Come again?"

"Food is a huge part of this event. I've got too many moving parts going on right now, and you're finished inviting people, right? Please, Yeardley. Would you take it?"

I did my best to look pathetic and needy. It would really be a huge weight off my shoulders if Yeardley agreed to help.

"Does Matt fall for that?" Yeardley pretended to be disgusted.

"I'm sure I don't know what you're talking about," I said, innocently batting my eyelashes.

"Fine. I'll do it. But only because I like the idea of working with Becky." Yeardley started to leave the room. "And you're not bad either, for a big sister." She grinned.

I smiled too, feeling lighter already. "Thank you, Yeardley."

This called for a celebration. Reaching for my phone, I speed dialed Matt.

"Hi, hon. How are you? What're you up to?"

"Hey. I was just thinking about you, and getting ready to watch the game." Matt muted the television before continuing. "So, a funny thing happened this morning. I went to the office to get ready for some stuff going on this week. When I walked past your office, Scott and Paul were in there."

"The president and vice president? What were they doing in my office? On a Sunday?"

"No idea but it looked like a pretty serious conversation was going down. And that's not all. I got an email from Martha in Human Resources. She wants to know when you'll be back."

"What did you tell her?"

"I said next Monday. Isn't that right?"

I stared out the window letting Matt's words sink in. The cottage's resident hummingbird was flitting about the red plastic feeder, a tiny bullet with blurred wings flapping. Burying its beak inside the feeder, the bird drank its fill of the container's syrupy solution then vanished into thin air.

"I don't know. I've been thinking a lot about Blue Sky Technologies. I really think I should go for the interview, don't you?" Before he could answer, I explained. "I thought I could take a couple more days off and tell work I was extending my vacation so I could fly to California early next week."

I could almost picture Matt sifting through my words and organizing them in his head. He spoke slowly. "So does that mean you've decided to go to California? What if Scott and Paul are preparing their own offer?"

Matt was an excellent sounding board. "Well, first off, I don't have an offer from California, yet." But I was pretty confident one was forthcoming. Blue Sky wouldn't make the investment in Ms. Bark's recruiting services, including the expense of bringing me out there, if they weren't fairly certain they wanted me. "And who knows what Scott and Paul are conspiring about. Maybe they plan to fire me when I get back." My heart froze at the thought. "You don't think they're going to fire me, do you, Matt?"

Matt's laugh was rich and deep. "Hardly, baby. You are the golden child around here right now. I'm expecting to see your name in lights over your office soon."

The doorbell rang and Matt broke away to answer it. "Shelby, I've gotta run. The boys are here to watch the game. Listen keep me posted on everything; the party, Nola and your sisters. And let me know what you plan to do about California. Something this big is important to both of us. Love you. Bye."

"Love you, too." I stared at the phone hoping he heard me.

MONDAY

Brown/Corliss

YEARDLEY

My stomach was in knots, driving to Greene's Market for the second time in as many days. The nervous anticipation of seeing Jackson again was making me crazy. It was the last thing I wanted. Or was it? I could deny it all I wanted, but I had to admit that some small traitorous part of me was secretly looking forward to it. I wondered whether I should thank Shelby or curse her for handing the catering duties over to me. But I couldn't be too hard on her; she was clearly in over her head.

That was a first. I had never seen this side of Shelby before, overwhelmed and asking for help. Selfishly, I found it kind of comforting to know that even my perfect sister suffered occasional moments of doubt. But right now she was just being silly. The party was going to be great. Maybe she was just missing Matt.

Shaking my head, I thought about the first time I met Matt. They had been dating less than a year. Matt had driven Shelby home to my parents' house for Christmas, planning on dropping her off on the way to see his own parents in Maine. Instead, he was sidelined by an unexpected blizzard. Stuck with us for the duration of the holidays, he had handled it like a trooper, totally charming us with his easy manner and healthy sense of fun.

"We've got this," he assured his Pictionary teammates, as Lily and I struggled to decipher his less than masterful stick drawings. We shrieked hysterically. He scribbled harder, for emphasis and even less clarity. "It's so obvious!"

It did not take a genius to understand Shelby's infatuation with 'the guy from the elevator' we had heard so much about. He was highly intelligent with a streak of dry humor that kept him clear of pompous. He was kind and sincere, good -looking and good-natured. The perfect complement to Shelby's consciously controlled overachiever. Matt and Dad had bonded over eggnog, concocting a special batch together. "Peach brandy is my secret ingredient," he had confided while my dad tutored him in the craft of properly folding the stiff egg whites into the liquid blend. Mom loved his sensitivity and appreciation for women in general, and her eldest daughter in particular.

Shelby practically glowed whenever he was in the same room. You would have to be ancient or dead not to feel the connection between them. My sister was head-over-heels in love and so was Matt.

Some girls have all the luck. I popped an Altoid in my mouth, savoring the cool heat of the melting mint, and thought of Jackson. As if summoned, his face showed clearly in the windshield, all dark gold curls, bronzed skin, and green cat eyes that saw right through me. His lips tilted in a lopsided smile, my favorite; the one that dared me to swim across the lake without waiting thirty minutes after eating, the one that made me laugh instead of smacking him for making me mad. It was the smile he wore the first time we slept together, his eyes locked on mine as his fingers fumbled nervously with my shirt buttons. Instantly, I smiled back. Old habits die hard.

I shook my head trying to erase the long-ago memory. We were just kids at that point, seventeen and eighteen, but I felt like I had known him forever. We had been friends for six summers, spending all or part of every day together swimming, water skiing, hanging out at the market. But that summer was different.

I remember once asking my mom how you know when you have met 'the one.' I figured a professor must have some pretty solid data on the subject. She smiled knowingly. I had asked the right person.

"I suppose it's different for everyone." She spoke slowly, choosing her words thoughtfully, like apples from a tree, taking only the perfect ones. "Daddy and I are certainly very different from each other, but we had chemistry and core."

"Core?"

"What we are inside. Our feelings, our beliefs, our thought processes. You see, the way a person shows themselves to the world is just an image, like a painting or a photograph. But if you really want to know what makes someone tick, what kind of person they are, you need to pay attention to what they do; actions are a demonstration of our core. You've heard the expression 'actions speak louder than words'? Well, that's what core means. At our cores, Dad and I are very similar people. Plus, he's so handsome," she added, making me blush. "It's as simple as that."

The parking lot at Greene's was packed when I pulled in, scouting for an open space amongst the chaos. The constant hustle and bustle of the place never ceased to amaze me. A car backed out leaving space for my Camry as I maneuvered between two large pickup trucks, *Greene's Market* painted in bold yellow letters on the sides. Bingo, front row. Any closer, I would be smack dab in the middle of Becky's kitchen.

Feeling lucky, I jumped from the car and marched confidently towards the market. Just outside, wooden produce tables laden with fruits and vegetables rested beneath a jaunty red and white striped awning. It flapped gently in the summer breeze, like sheets on a clothesline. I paused inside, closing my eyes and breathing deeply. Mother Nature's fruity perfume, blended with the warm aroma of fresh baked breads and pastries, was intoxicating.

Something brushed my arm. "Can I help you find something, or are you going on blind faith?"

My eyes flew open as I clutched a hand to my chest.

"Jesus, Jackson, you scared the shit out of me!" Crossing my arms tightly, I hid my pounding heart from view. "Do you treat all your customers that way?"

A broad smile split his face, like the sun coming out from a cloud. I felt my blood warm.

"Just the special ones. But I don't see anyone complaining." He pointed to the masses wandering happily through the aisles, filling their baskets with everything from the basics to regional specialties. I had to agree. They came from near and far to shop at Greene's. Some things never change.

"Everything changes eventually," Jackson countered, reading my mind with a warm, probing gaze that made my toes curl in delight. He was right. I did not recognize the guy standing in front me. Once a lanky teenager, Jackson was a grown man now.

He excused himself to assist a customer. I stared unabashedly at Jackson's broad shoulders filling out the cotton t-shirt he wore like a second skin. Jackson's biceps flexed mightily as he lifted a case of beer into a nearby shopping carriage. He straightened, proving he was even taller than I remembered. Six two, at least. But it was his face that had changed most of all. The soft curves of adolescence were gone. Shed along with the past, they had been replaced by an Erector set of precise angles and planes; a classic Roman nose, firm jaw, and strong chin.

"Sorry about that," he apologized, throwing a thumb in the direction he had just come from, and bringing my daydreaming to an abrupt halt. "Are you here to see my mom?"

"Yeah. Shelby asked if I would take the catering for Nola's party off her plate. No pun intended."

"Wow. That doesn't sound like the Shelby I remember."

"I know, right?" With a sigh, I followed him to the back of the store where Becky was probably already up to her elbows in preparations.

"So it looks like I'll be spending some time here over the next few days. I hope you don't mind."

Jackson stopped and turned mid-stride, catching my face with his chest. I stayed there, breathing him in until he gently pushed me away.

"Why would I mind?" He looked genuinely puzzled.

My face burned beet red. "Well, you know." Digging my hands into my pockets, I wished the ground would just swallow me up. "Because we dated."

I forced myself to look at him, his eyes still murky with confusion. "And then we didn't. So I promise, I won't get in your way while I'm here."

Dropping my eyes to the floor, I concentrated on the touch of his hands. They were warm and calloused on my arms. He squeezed them gently, and I lifted my gaze to meet his.

"Yeardley." He said my name like a question, his head tilted to one side as he studied my face intently. "Is that what you think? We're not friends anymore?"

He released me, and took a step back, scratching his head in bemusement.

"No! I mean, I don't know." Now who was confused? "It's been a long time, you know," I finished lamely.

He nodded, silently agreeing. "Yeah, I guess it has."

For a moment neither of us moved, rooted in place by our thoughts until Jackson cleared his throat. Smiling politely, he motioned for me to follow him.

"C'mon, I'll take you to the kitchen now. Mom's probably wondering where you are."

YEARDLEY

"It's all in the wrist, Yeardley," Becky coached from across the counter. "Like this."

I watched as she used her wrists to power the pads of her hands into a mound of dough, flipping it lightly with her fingertips, and repeating.

"Knead and flip, knead and flip. That's how you do it," she smiled.

I followed her instructions closely, pounding and tossing a lump of soon-to-be dinner rolls.

"Is something wrong, dear?" she asked, watching me with growing concern.

"Not at all."

On the contrary, helping Becky cook for the party was making the afternoon fly by. Whisking marinades and pounding dough were excellent distractions. They kept me from thinking about other things. Like Jackson. My former friend. Or so it seemed. He certainly did not say anything to make me think otherwise. I ground my hands into the dough, picturing his face, and smiled. That felt good.

So did spending time with his mother. Our 'summer aunt,' my sisters and I called her. After Nola, she was the person we loved most in Shepardsville, and not just because she made our favorite pies whenever we asked. Nola and Becky had been best friends forever, sharing everything over the years from clothes and makeup to advice and recipes. It was only natural, Nola said, that she would share us with her best friend, too. Surrogate daughters so to speak since Becky and Bob never had any of their own. They were completely devoted to Jackson.

Becky did not have a mean bone in her body, and here I was, beating on her tender dough. Feeling guilty, I gentled my touch and changed the subject.

"You've made a lot of changes around here," I said, bobbing my chin towards the swinging kitchen doors and the store beyond them. "A build-your-own salad bar and a petting zoo."

"And a gift shop showcasing jewelry and other accessories made by local artists," Becky beamed. "We're selling out faster than we can stock it. But Bob and I can't take credit for any of it. It's all Jackson's doing, with a little help from his business degree. Now I know why we never had more kids. One college tuition was all we could handle."

I thought of the six main registers with the steady stream of paying customers flowing through them and thought it highly doubtful that money was an issue. The market seemed even busier than I remembered. The result of Jackson's hard work no doubt.

"He went to the University of Rochester, right?" I asked conversationally, knowing full well the answer was yes.

It was all the encouragement Becky needed to launch into a full-length dissertation on her favorite subject. Jackson had graduated summa cum laude and had his pick of corporate job offers to choose from. He chose to come home and run the family business instead. Since then, Jackson had been pouring all of his time and energy into expanding the market. It was obviously paying off, but his parents sometimes wondered if it was too much, if he had made the right decision. Jackson was a young man. He needed a life. He needed a woman. Becky looked pointedly at me.

I blushed. Burying my hands in a fresh batch of dough, I wondered whatever happened to the girlfriend I had met my last summer at the lake. Something bitter coated my tongue, and I took a sip of water.

She had been tall and blonde and beautiful as she stood in *my* spot next to Jackson. With one arm wrapped tightly around Jackson's waist, she looked glued to him as his arm draped casually over her shoulders.

"Hey, Yeardley," Jackson had greeted me with a friendly smile, before introducing me to Blondie. "This is my friend, Yeardley. She and her sisters have been spending summers here with their aunt for as long as any of us can remember. They're practically family."

Friend. Family. Had he really used those words to describe me? A punch in the gut would have hurt less. I couldn't believe it. Not after last summer.

It had taken everything I had not to throw up then and there. Instead, I pasted a sick smile on my face, and extended my hand to her. "Hi, nice to meet you. Will you be visiting long?" *Please God, no.*

"Any friend of Jack's is a friend of mine," she had replied, ignoring my hand and my question. Blondie hugged me. "It's so nice to meet you, Yeardley."

Her soft, silky hair covered her shoulder, tickling my chin. Choking in her embrace, I had looked to Jackson for help, but he'd only had eyes for Blondie.

"Jack's told me so much about you. It's a shame we won't get to spend more time together. We're leaving tomorrow." Grabbing Jackson's hand, she smiled brilliantly, "Jack's staying with me at my parents' horse farm in Virginia this summer. Daddy's going to teach him a thing or two about the stud business. Not that he needs much coaching," she giggled.

I glanced at Jackson. He was blushing, but beaming, too, proud as a peacock.

Remembering it like yesterday, I took another sip of water. Perspiration pricked my forehead. *Jack* and his new girlfriend. My stomach twisted in a painful knot. The same gut-wrenching sensation that had cohabitated with my broken heart, and tortured me for the rest of that interminable summer.

"Maybe we should call it a day," Becky suggested, interrupting my thoughts as she moved to wash her hands at the sink. "You've been a huge help, but you're only here for the week. I can't be hogging all of your time. Go catch up with your friends. Visit with Nola. I imagine there are a lot of people you want to see while you're here."

She dried her hands on a towel and came to stand beside me. "And people who want to see you too." Her green eyes twinkled. "Now go," she shooed. "Go have some fun. This will all be here tomorrow." She spread her arms wide, promising more work to come.

I checked my watch and shrugged. "If you're sure. You know I still have plenty of time before happy hour with Nola and my sisters. I wish you'd let me do something. You and Bob are doing so much for this party that we just sprang on you."

"Nonsense. Go, get out of here." Becky pushed me through the swinging doors into the congestion of shopping traffic.

Like walking from a dark room into light, it took me a second to adjust from the calm order of Becky's kitchen to the shopping frenzy happening around me. The familiar sights and sounds enveloped me like a favorite old sweater, comfy and cozy. Reluctantly, I made my way back to the car.

Using the remote to unlock the car, I set its lights flashing

"Don't you trust us?" From the other side of the Camry, Jackson mocked me with that damn crooked smile. I had not seen him approach.

I shifted uneasily. "What do you mean?"

"This is the safest place in America. Around here, we don't lock our homes much less our cars." His eyes crinkled, teasing me.

I shrugged, relaxing my shoulders ever so slightly. "Yeah, well, not so much in Boston."

We smiled at each other across the Camry. I could feel my guard slipping. Before it disappeared completely, I reached for the door handle. "Okay, see you later."

"Wait, where're you going?"

Good question. Since getting kicked out of the kitchen, I hadn't really thought about it. Ruth would not be back in town for a few days yet.

"Back to the cottage." *Where no one will hurt me.* "I feel like going for a swim."

He nodded, staring hard at the ground. When he finally looked up, I almost wished he hadn't. Without a smile, his face seemed sad. I clenched my hands, resisting the urge to reach out. *He needs a life.* His mom's words whispered in my ear.

"How about going for a ride? With me." He nodded his head toward his truck. "I have to pick up some more corn from Stone's farm. A little company would be nice."

I was burning up despite the cool breeze blowing on my neck. "I don't know." I hesitated, uncertain.

"Scared?" He taunted, openly laughing at me now. "I promise, I won't bite."

I had heard that before. Years ago, on a moonless night, we were hidden from view of the cottage where my nosy sisters peered futilely through the windows. Side by side, Jackson and I had laid on the grass, holding hands and facing each other. Our eyes were the only things shining in the velvety darkness.

Speaking in hushed tones, Jackson whispered, "I want to be with you, Yeardley, more than anything."

I nodded, feeling the same. "Me too. Really," I promised, sensing his doubt. "Really." I squeezed his hand tight. "I'm just...scared."

In the dark, his green eyes glowed bright with surprise. "Don't you trust me? I swear, I'd never do anything to hurt you," he vowed, solemn as an altar boy.

Much as I wanted to believe him, I couldn't help thinking of the books Ruth and I had secretly snuck out of the library. They were stashed under her mattress for safekeeping. Statistically speaking, a girl's first time wasn't usually that great. It could even be painful sometimes.

Swallowing hard, I rolled closer, pressing my lips firmly against his, mustering up courage I didn't yet have. "I'm sorry, Jackson. I want you too. But I need more time." I shifted away, anticipating his disappointment.

"Hey, come back here." His voice was firm but soft. He rolled on top of me. Taking my face in his hands, he touched his lips to mine in a feathery kiss. "You're not ready yet. That's fine. I'll wait, for as long as you need me to."

His lips twitched as if laughing at some private joke. "But until then, is it okay if I kiss you like this?" His warm tongue probed the depths of my mouth stealing my breath away. "And if I touch you like this?" His hands slid slowly beneath my shirt up the length of my waist to fondle my bare breasts. Lowering his head, his teeth grazed the tender skin of my neck, sending shivers up my spine. Feeling me quiver, Jackson lifted his dark gaze to mine and promised: "Don't worry. I won't bite."

Jackson cleared his throat, bringing me back to the present. He was waiting for an answer.

"I suppose I could take a quick ride. The lake will still be here when we get back."

Rewarding me with a smile, he waved his arm, guiding me to the truck. "Alrighty then, let's go."

The Ford F150 powered its way up the rolling hills of Route 21 to Stone's Farm. To my right and far below, the lake sparkled like a giant sapphire set amongst a ring of tree-topped hills and sloping valleys.

"I'd forgotten how beautiful it is," I breathed, swept away by the arresting sight.

"Me too."

I flashed him a smile but Jackson was focused on the road ahead. I understood what he meant though.

"I suppose we're all guilty of that, taking for granted what's right in front of us. Boston is a great city, but the only time I really take advantage of everything it has to offer is when I have out-of-town guests visiting." Gazing out the window again I vowed, "If I lived here, I swear I'd never take any of it for granted."

"Do you think the city mouse could be happy as a country mouse?" Jackson joked, his look anything but teasing. "Things aren't quite as exciting around here, you know."

"Maybe. But excitement comes in all shapes and sizes. What I do know is that I have spent so much of my life, too much, searching for something." I shook my head, answering Jackson's unasked question. "I don't know what. But waiting around to see what tomorrow will bring is getting pretty old. Not to mention lonely."

The words were out before I could stop them. I clamped my lips together before any more could escape. Why was I telling him all this?

Silently digesting our conversation, Jackson let his gaze wash over me like a searchlight. I tried to see myself through his eyes. Brightly painted toes splashed color on my feet and tan, bare legs. I wore cut off jeans, frayed at the edges with a white scoop neck t-shirt that barely hinted at the cleavage between modestly rounded breasts. My cheeks were rosy from the sun and lightly freckled. Not bad. I challenged him to say otherwise.

"Didn't see that coming," he said, blessing me with my favorite smile. "What happened to Yeardley Lane, the human magnet? You'd meet someone new and thirty seconds later they'd be telling you their life story, juicy details and all. Sometimes it was too much information. People are just naturally drawn to you."

Something warm burst inside me, turning my rosy cheeks red. I hugged a knee to my chest, embracing the heady feel of his words: a human magnet. Not resume material perhaps, but it did wonders for my soul.

"I never thought of it that way. Maybe you're right. Still, it's possible to be surrounded by people and still be lonely. I guess I need my own magnet, someone *I* want to be around."

I felt him glance at my left hand. "So, no husband or fiancé? Boyfriend?"

I shook my head. "You?"

"Hard to believe, I know, but no." He grinned, raising his hand for protection from my scolding slap. "Ouch!"

"Baby." I gave him a reproachful look. "So what about Blondie, not in the picture anymore?"

"Who?"

"Oh come on, *Jack*, you remember. Miss Tell Me About It Stud from the great state of Virginia."

Jackson's laughter boomed, filling the cab with good humor. This was fun, two friends catching up and talking about old times.

"You mean Lorelei? God, I haven't thought of her in years." A wistful look turned his eyes smoky green. "She was a beauty."

I smacked his arm again, bringing him back to Earth, and demanded to know, "So she wasn't the love of your life?"

"What?" He had the grace to look startled. "Lorelei was great, but no," Jackson shook his head in emphasis. "Not my dream girl."

I pondered that for a moment, gearing up to ask his idea of the perfect woman, when he spoke again.

"Here we are, Stone's Farm. Remember the year we took sailing lessons and Rick Jr. was in our class? He's the top dog now, running the whole operation since his folks retired to Florida. Come say hi. This won't take long."

Jackson jumped out of the truck and was at my door before I had unbuckled my seatbelt. Taking his hand, I jumped off the running board. Our eyes met briefly before he dropped my hand. Turning, he led the way to Rick's office.

"I brought a visitor," Jackson announced stepping to one side so Rick could see me clearly. "Look familiar?"

With a few taps on the keyboard to save his work, Rick pushed away from his computer. He stood to greet his guests. "Hey, Jackson, how goes it?"

Finished shaking hands, he turned to see the mystery visitor. "Yeardley Lane. Wow. What happened to the skinny little sailor girl I used to know? She's a real Boston beauty now, don't you think, Jackson?"

Jackson frowned and Rick laughed. "You know I love my wife. I'm just admiring an old friend here."

Laughing, I gave him a hug, stepping back for a once-over of my own. A few years older than Jackson and me, Rick was still holding his own with a full head of thick dark hair. From the tell tale lines showing white against his deeply tanned neck, I could tell his hair was freshly trimmed. Clusters of laugh lines fanned from his eyes like good-humored sunbursts. I smiled back as he patted the small mound beneath his checkered button down shirt. Seems like Rick still had a thing for king size candy bars.

"Hey, Rick, it's good to see you again. So this is your place now?"

"It is." Sounding like the man in charge, Rick asked Jackson, "You need more corn? I can have the boys fill the truck while we catch up."

At Jackson's nod, he pulled a walkie-talkie from his pants pocket and spoke into it. "Hey, Scott, Greene's Market is here for a fill up. Get a couple of guys on it, will you?" An answering voice confirmed the order, and Rick signed off. "Thanks."

"They're taking care of it," he said to Jackson before turning his attention back to me. "So what brings you back to town, Yeardley? It's been a long time."

Bringing Rick up to speed, I told him all about Nola's invitation to me and my sisters and our spontaneous return to the lake. "And now we're planning a huge birthday bash for her at the end of the week. I hope you and your wife will come."

I felt bad inviting them after the fact, but Rick didn't seem to notice. "Sure we will. Annie's pregnant and out of her mind waiting for the baby to come. This'll be a good distraction."

The walkie-talkie squawked that the truck was full and Rick escorted us outside. We waved our good byes as Jackson reversed the truck, steering it back onto the road.

We drove in comfortable silence for a while, lost in our thoughts and enjoying the view. Winding our way past vineyards and orchards, we passed acres of open fields spotted with deer, grazing undisturbed. The road sloped down towards the lake and hugged the shore. Glimpses of sparkling water splashed at us like rain drops through the leafy trees lining the road. I frowned, confused.

"This isn't the way back to the market."

Lifting his eyes from the road, Jackson looked at me and agreed. "Nice to see you still know your way around here."

Turning left, we drove down a dirt road through a tunnel of trees, a glimmer of light shining at its end. It was a cottage, a real one, small and welcoming, with Adirondack chairs and a fire pit on a postage stamp of green grass. In front, a pebbled beach, private and obscure, shared its space with a neon-colored kayak and a paddleboard. A standard issue dock stretched out into the water.

"Where are we?" I asked, drinking it all in.

"My place."

I shifted towards him, catching a glimpse of myself in the rearview mirror. I looked as confused as I felt. "Since when? I mean, don't you live with your parents?"

"I bought it a couple of years ago," he explained. "My parents are great and all, but my old room was getting a little small. Plus, I converted one of the bedrooms here into an office so I can work any time, night or day. And there's a kitchen with a dining nook, a small living room, and a porch with a swing. Everything I need, for the most part."

The cottage was perfect in every way. It was easy to see why he loved it. "But what are we doing here?" I asked, sensing something was up.

"You wanted to go for a swim, didn't you?" He waved his arm, palm up, offering the lake for my inspection. "Take it from me, this is the best swimming spot on the entire west lake."

I laughed. "If you do say so yourself."

Hopping out of the truck, we walked to the beach and let the water lap at our toes. I pictured myself jumping in, the silky water gliding over my skin, my arms like knives cutting through the surface.

"I can't go swimming," I moaned, my wonderful daydream shattered. "I don't have my suit."

"Since when has that been a problem?"

Jackson's voice was low and seductive, and dangerous. He grabbed his t-shirt, pulling it over his head and shoulders, revealing the toned landscape of his naked torso beneath. My breath stuck in my throat as my eyes raced across the terrain of his bronzed chest. His flat abs rippled across his rib cage, not an ounce of fat on him. I swallowed hard, keeping my composure.

"Ready?" He dared, his crooked smile silently challenging. Infuriating me.

"Whenever you are," I glared, keeping my eyes on his as I stripped down to my underwear. The light in Jackson's eyes smoldered to an appreciative glow.

"What's the matter, never seen a girl naked before?" Feeling smug, I kicked off my flip-flops.

A moment later, my feet were in the air, my knees braced from behind by the steel grip of Jackson's arm. Another arm wrapped firmly around my back as Jackson carried me to the end of the dock.

"Shut up and swim." He tossed me into the lake like a sack of flour, diving in after me.

I spluttered to the surface and spotted him, floating like an otter, with his arms folded behind his head, his boxer clad legs extended.

"Fine."

I swam away from the cottage, setting course for a neighboring float a few houses away. Breathe and stroke. Breathe and stroke. Breathe and stroke. Just like the pool back home, only a thousand times better. I propelled myself forward, closing in on my target. Jackson caught up to me, matching me stroke for stroke until we reached the float. Clinging to the side, we bobbed weightless in the water, and caught our breath.

"Thank you," I smiled, forgetting I was mad at him. "I can die happy now."

With a flat hand, he tapped gently against his ear as if unblocking it, a wicked grin plastered on his face.

"Thank *you*. That's high praise coming from a naked woman."

Opening my mouth to retort, I shut it again, lost for words. Jackson swam away, leaving me to follow, or not. As if I had a choice. Something tugged on my heartstrings and I sighed, helpless against its pull. Slipping into an easy breaststroke, I made my way back to Jackson waiting patiently for me on the beach. This was going to be a very long week.

LILY

I felt so alive motoring around Shepardsville in our economy rental. It was a far cry from my Mercedes. Then again, I was a long way from Miami. Everything was different here. It always had been.

This place had shaped me. I became an artist here, inspired by the color palette of the lake, the hills, the sunrises and sunsets. Inspiration was all around me, giving me a style all my own.

"I can't put my finger on it," Diego said to me shortly after we met.

It was just the two of us at dinner. Diego had rented out the entire restaurant. Already my employer, he was pulling out all the stops to get me into his bed.

"There is something about you. Different. Rare."

With a butterfly's touch, Diego traced a question mark on my skin. Goosebumps followed in his wake.

"Where did you come from, Lily Lane?" He asked softly, pressing his lips to mine.

Diego had swept me off my feet that night. Wine and romance will do that. But it was more than that. Diego had seen something in me that few had ever recognized. I was a Canandaigua girl.

The air conditioning blasted in the car. I shivered, dialing it back to moderate strength. No time for brain freeze. I had to focus.

Turning down Jib Way on the 23 Street Loop, I tried to remember which house belonged to Mrs. Rollins. Mrs. Rollins was a master gardener. When I told her about Nola's party, she insisted on making the floral arrangements herself, from her own expansive flower gardens.

In short order, I spotted Mrs. Rollins' home. It was a small weathered cottage marked by a lone oak tree, deeply rooted at the end of the driveway. A small sign hung from the tree: Koanella. I was in the right place. If the sign didn't convince me, the elegant gardens gracing the front lawn certainly did.

There were raised beds of petunias, marigolds and impatiens. Bushes of hydrangea, lilac, and Rose of Sharon grew resplendent with white, purple and pink blossoms. Mrs. Rollins' container gardens were bursting with red Salvia, green Dusty miller, and purple Heather placed strategically around the yard. I parked the car and started walking towards the house.

"Lily!" Mrs. Rollins called my name. "Over here, by the sun flowers."

I strained to see her. Wearing a yellow dress with green crocs and a wide-brimmed straw hat, Mrs. Rollins bore a striking resemblance to the bright floral stalks she was tending. Spotting her at last, I made my way over to greet her.

"Lily!" Mrs. Rollins shrieked, pulling me close for a hug. "You're here." Holding me at arm's length, she exclaimed, "I haven't seen you in forever. How long has it been?"

I beamed at her. Mrs. Rollins' enthusiasm was contagious. "It's been too long, Mrs. Rollins, too long. But just in time to celebrate Nola's big birthday. Let's talk flowers, shall we?"

An hour later I emerged from Mrs. Rollins' house smelling like roses and lavender. If her centerpieces looked half as good as I smelled, Nola's party was certain to be a Garden of Eden.

My next stop was Cardinal Crafts, for party favors. In Miami, you didn't leave an opening, or a fashion show, or a party without some swag. Nola's guests would not go home empty-handed either. The search was on for that special trinket that would forever remind them of Nola's special night.

I stepped inside, pausing a moment to soak it all in. Just like the merchandise, Cardinal Crafts was unique. Once a barn, it had been converted to retail space, a place with country store charm and appeal.

"May I help you?" A female voice called to me.

Following the sound, I turned to see a petite woman with a warm smile standing behind the counter. She did not look familiar to me. No surprise. *You're the visitor here now*, I reminded myself sadly.

"I think you can," I smiled, joining her at the counter. "I am planning a lakefront extravaganza on very short notice. I need a million things to make it happen."

"Only a million?" Her eyes crinkled at my request. "Well, you've come to the right place. Cardinal Crafts is party central. Tell me about your event."

"It's a birthday celebration for my aunt," I explained. "Sixty-five years, every one of them right here in Shepardsville. My sisters and I want to throw a wonderful party for one of the most wonderful women we know."

The woman nodded, encouraging me to continue.

"We've decided on a retro chic lake theme. Outdoor elegance laced with tradition. Does that make sense?" I crossed my fingers. Shepardsville might not be Miami, but I was pretty sure it could hold its own in the social arena.

"Of course. I know exactly the effect you're striving for. We have so many wonderful things here in the store that just scream retro chic. If you don't mind me asking, who is your aunt? I've lived here a long time myself. Maybe I know her."

"Nola Hamilton."

"Oh my goodness!" she exclaimed. "Nola teaches technology classes with my daughter Kathleen at the Adult Exchange."

"The Adult Exchange?"

"Yes, at the library where Nola works. It's a course for adults to get savvy about technology. They meet one night a week. Nola and Kathleen show the class how to use computers and smart phones and such."

I was quiet, listening as the woman continued to explain.

"You know, it took a long time for technology to come to this area. Sometimes the folks who live here year round need a little help getting up to speed. My Kathleen just adores Nola."

I extended my hand to the tiny woman. "Well, your daughter and I have that in common. I'm Lily Lane. My sisters Shelby, Yeardley and I used to spend summers here as kids. We don't get back here as often as we'd like anymore, but we really want to make the most of the time we have now. The party is this coming Saturday. It's short notice, but do you think you can help me out?"

She grasped my hand in hers. "It's so nice to meet you, Lily. I'm Sheila Cavendish." Our introductions complete, we went to work.

"I'm sure we have everything you need for the perfect party."

Sheila gestured for me to join her at a round table covered with magazines, decoration samples, and books.

"Dig in. Let's see if we can find some inspiration."

Using my own sketches as guides, we flipped through page after page of decorative materials, choosing products to match my designs. Twinkle lights and lanterns and sparklers. Canoe shakers and rafia wrapped utensils and signature party favors. Nola's party was going to be nothing short of spectacular.

"Sheila, you are amazing! *This* was amazing." I waved a hand between us. "We make a great team. Thank you for all your help."

Sheila nodded her agreement. "It was fun, but exhausting. I don't know how you're still standing when I'm ready for bed." She laughed.

"I'm a little pooped too," I confessed. "I think party planning is even more challenging than interior design. But I can't wait to see Nola's face when she sees what we have accomplished."

"Me too. Thank you for the invitation. Kathleen and I wouldn't miss this party for the world."

"Excellent. I'll see you there."

I left the store, feeling exuberant. The party was coming together perfectly. Jumping in the car, I pointed it in the direction of the cottage. It was time to update the girls.

TUESDAY

Brown/Corliss

SHELBY

I collapsed into bed with one of Nola's reading selections in my hand. I didn't even know what book it was. It didn't really matter. Nola knew what I liked. The important thing was I finally had time to read something besides project schedules, program code sheets, and security analysis data. With a sigh of contentment, I sank into my pillows. Lovely.

"Hey, Shel?" Lily's damp head poked around my bedroom door. "Watcha doin?"

Plopping herself at the end of my bed, Lily grabbed the book from my hand and tossed it out of reach. "I'm bored," she complained.

"Lily, how can you be bored? You're at the lake." I could think of a million things she could do to entertain herself. None of them included keeping me from escaping into the pages of a good book. "Why don't you go for a swim? It's almost a full moon. It should be bright enough."

Folding her legs like a pretzel, Lily made herself comfortable on the bed. "I already did that." She pointed to her wet hair. "I even went skinny dipping like we used to do. But it's no fun all alone."

Squirming slightly under Lily's accusing stare, I refused to surrender. "Where's Yeardley? She's always up for swimming. She'll go with you."

"Yeah, if she was here," Lily pouted. "She's out with Jackson somewhere."

Guess I wasn't meant to read tonight after all. Patting the space next to me, I motioned for Lily to join me. "Looks like it's just us then," I sighed, pulling the blanket lightly over our legs.

"What do you think is going on with those two?" Lily asked, doing nothing to disguise her curiosity. "They've been practically inseparable since she started helping Becky with the party catering."

Lily was right about that. When we were younger, if you wanted to know where Yeardley was, you just had to look for Jackson, and vise versa. Ten years later, it seemed they had slipped back into their old ways once again.

"Well, she can thank me later for turning the catering duties over to her," I said dryly.

Lily giggled. Clasping her hands behind her head, she stared dreamily at the ceiling. "What about you, Shelby? We've been here four days now. I think that's the longest you and Matt have been apart since you met. How are you holding up?"

"I miss him, of course. But I've got you guys." I poked Lily's arm affectionately. "We should do sister time more often."

Reaching down the length of the bed, I grabbed the book Lily had left there and placed it on the nightstand. "Besides, I'm going to have to get used to not seeing Matt for a little bit longer." I turned to Lily. "Can you keep a secret?"

"Not once in her twenty-five years," proclaimed Yeardley, back from her outing with Jackson. "But I can." From the doorway she asked, "Can I come in too?"

Lily and I waved her in, and Yeardley bounded across the room to the bottom of my bed. I tossed her a pillow as she wrapped herself in one of Nola's hand-knitted afghans. "So, what did I miss? What's the secret?"

"Shelby was just about to tell us why she won't be seeing Matt for a while," Lily explained. "The floor's yours, Shelby."

I looked at my sisters waiting eagerly for me to confide in them. Their faces were bright with excitement. I hated to disappoint them. "It's not that exciting, guys." But actually, to me, it was. "I was contacted by a head hunter just before I came to the lake. She wants me to meet with her client, the number one tech firm on the West Coast."

"Oh my gosh, Shelby. That's amazing."

"Congratulations, big sister." Sitting up on her knees, Yeardley high-fived me.

It felt good to tell them the news; the two people I had shared all of my secrets with before Matt came along. "Thanks, guys." I beckoned my sisters closer. "Group hug, please."

We settled ourselves back into bed. "I don't get it. What's that got to do with seeing Matt?" Yeardley was confused.

"I'm thinking I might fly direct from here to San Francisco on Sunday," I explained. "That gives me time to rest up and get ready for an interview early next week. *If* they can meet with me then, it would be easier to 'extend my vacation,'" I air quoted, "than go back to work and suddenly take more time off."

Yeardley agreed with me. "Sounds like you've got it all figured out. So does this mean you want to move to California?"

I'd been asking myself the same thing ever since I got the call from Hillary Bark. "I don't know yet. I don't know what the position is or even what company it is for sure. There's a lot to think about."

"What does Matt think?" Lily had been sitting quietly listening to our conversation.

"He's excited for me. And proud," I said, blushing a little. "He knows this is an incredible opportunity for me."

"You mean for both of you." Lily looked at me, unblinking.

Surprised, it took me a moment to answer her. "Of course, it's a great opportunity for both of us. Why wouldn't it be?"

"No reason," Lily shrugged. "It's just that you're the one with the job interview, not Matt. Will he go with you if you decide to move out there? Didn't you guys just buy a place?"

Lily's questions sliced clean to the core as I tried hard to remember my conversations with Matt. He had been happy for me. Definitely. He was supportive of me. Absolutely. We had talked only about me. Oh, shit!

"Oh my God." I looked at Lily and Yeardley, panicked. "We've never talked about what this means for us. I didn't even think about it. Matt is everything to me."

Yeardley squeezed my foot gently. "Tell him that."

"Even if he already knows," Lily added. "If Matt means that much to you, you have to include him in your decision. Your life isn't the only one that's about to change."

I looked at my baby sister speaking words of wisdom beyond her years. Out of the mouths of babes.

LILY

I slipped off my rings, and placed them carefully on the bathroom counter. The hand cream felt refreshing as I massaged it into my skin. My mind started to wander. Shelby was so lucky to have a guy like Matt. I knew he was perfect for her the minute I met him. My instincts said Matt would follow Shelby wherever she went, but this was the kind of decision they would have to make together.

As I flipped off the bathroom light and made my way down the hall to my bedroom, I thought about Diego. If I had a job opportunity somewhere else, would he follow me? Of course not, I argued with myself. He'd help me pack my bags and he may even shed a tear or two. He was never going to relocate Alverez Designs, and quite frankly, I did not blame him.

"Baby," he would coo into my ear. "Don't go. Stay here with me and be my partner... my lover." He would rub my shoulders with his soft hands. "Let's show Miami how great we are together."

"But, Diego," I would say, letting him massage the tension from my neck. "I need to make my own mark on the design world. You of all people should understand. You did the same thing with your company."

Diego could be very persistent. "That's right, my darling. I've done all the hard work already. Stay here and be by my side. Someone as beautiful as you should only have to be cherished. Why do you want to do all that work? Just stay with me and let me spoil you."

No one could spoil me quite like Diego. I was not sure I wanted to give that up. Caroline thought I was crazy to be restless. She understood the office gossip got under my skin but she thought I should rise above it.

"Fight back by being the best designer in this firm, Lily. You don't owe any of these others an explanation about your relationship with Diego. They're going to talk; that's the way an office works. Just rise above it."

I pulled the covers back and climbed into the bed. Even though it had been a very long time, the softness of the mattress and the smell of clean sheets brought me right back to being a young girl.

"You sleeping?" A soft voiced called from my doorway. I lifted my head from the pillow in time to see Yeardley's face in the dim light from my open windows.

"Just got into bed." I murmured, already feeling sleepy. "What's up?"

"Nothing. I can't sleep. I just came from Shelby's room and she's snoring. I wonder if Matt knows she snores like a bear when she's really tired?"

"I have to believe that he must know, Yeardley. They've been living together a while now. You can't hide something like snoring." I sat up in bed and pulled the covers back. "Diego snores whenever he's had too much wine."

Yeardley scampered in and jumped on my bed. "Really? What else does Diego do when he's had too much wine?" She had the most ridiculous grin on her face.

"I'm not telling you anything!"

"Oh, come on, Lily! You used to tell me everything about your old boyfriends."

"Yeah, well that train has left the station, dear sister. Besides, I want to know what's going on between you and Jackson." I grinned right back at her.

"Nothing," Yeardley said quickly, looking at the floor.

"Oh, come on!" I shook her arm until she looked back at me. "You're not going to get off that easily. It looks like someone is picking right back up where she left off many years ago."

"I don't know," Yeardley's voice trailed off.

"Do you still have feelings for him, Yeardley? You used to be so close when we were kids. I remember the two of you moved in tandem all summer."

"It feels so good. I've forgotten how much I love spending time with him. But Lily, he's a grown man now. I have no idea what to think, and let's face it; I'm only here for a week."

I realized this was my opportunity to make up for my critical remarks from the other night.

"Hey, Yeardley, sometimes things can't be planned. We're always goofing all over Shelby because she's so organized and everything is planned. You are at your best when you just let life take its course. Don't worry about only being here a week. Enjoy every minute of being with Jackson. Take a chance."

Yeardley looked at me gratefully. "Thanks, sis. I think I will." She reached over and gave me a bear hug.

I looked at Yeardley's happy face. I loved my sisters and this week made me realize how much I missed them.

"Now get out!" I exclaimed feigning disgust. "I need my beauty sleep."

Yeardley climbed off the bed. "Do you ever!" She slipped out the door before I could reply.

WEDNESDAY

YEARDLEY

Hail pelted against the windows, softly at first but growing louder, insistent, commanding me to wake up. The room was dark, but light enough to see the hazy silhouette of the ceiling fan, whirring in lazy circles above my bed. With a yawning stretch, I went to the window. The rising sun was barely peeping above the horizon. Jackson was on the lawn below, getting ready to launch another handful of pebbles at my window.

"I'm awake. Be down in a second," I whispered, not bothering to see if he had heard me before I went to get dressed.

Trading my nightshirt for khaki shorts and a t-shirt, I made my way to the bathroom, washing quickly. Downstairs, I grabbed a banana and a bottle of water from the kitchen, and let myself out of the cottage quietly, careful not to slam the screen door behind me. I trotted across the dewy grass to the idling truck. Jackson waited until I was buckled in before handing me a cup of coffee. Hot and sweet. Just like him.

This pre-dawn ritual had become our routine, ever since Lily and Shelby had commandeered the use of both Nola's car and our rental. Finding myself stranded with no way of getting to Greene's, I had called Becky to explain my predicament.

"I'm sure Nola won't mind if I use her kitchen to cook for the party. What do you want me to make?"

Becky was having none of it. "No way. Nola will start meddling. Before you know it, she'll be taking over and pushing you out the door."

I could almost hear her frowning over the phone. "Jackson will come get you," she said emphatically, as if sensing my objection. "I won't take no for an answer."

So here we were, driving and sipping our coffees, gearing up for another day at the market. The parking lot was empty when we got there. Greene's did not open for another hour, but we could see lights shining from the kitchen. Becky was making donuts and muffins for the morning coffee crowd.

Bob moved through the front of the store, a phone stuck to his ear. He was pushing a small cart stacked with cash drawers, and stopping to load them into their proper registers.

"Here they come now." He looked up and winked as Jackson and I walked into the store. "Okay, I'll tell her." He grinned into the phone. "Yeah. I'll tell her that, too."

"Morning." Jackson and I greeted him in unison.

"Good morning. Looks like another beautiful day," He pointed to the sun shining brightly outside.

"Yeardley, that was Nola on the phone. She'd like you to bring a pie home tonight. Chocolate chip for Princess Lily."

I nodded, and walked towards the kitchen.

"Oh, and she said to tell you the doorbell works just fine. Always has." He looked at me, puzzled. "Am I missing some kind of joke here?"

Jackson's eyes grew big as saucers, his sheepish expression mirroring my own. Clearly, we had underestimated Nola. I blamed Jackson, of course. It was his idea to reinstate our old calling system. We had devised this system years ago when the doorbell just would not do, such as late night rendezvous, long after my aunt and sisters had gone to bed. I would lie in bed, pretending to sleep, and wait for the sound of pebbles pinging on my window. Under the cover of darkness, Jackson and I would slip away, sometimes meeting up with friends, sometimes to be alone in secret, but not as secret as we had thought apparently.

Jackson grinned as our past caught up to us. How dumb were we thinking we could get anything past Nola. I shrugged, chalking it up to youthful naiveté.

"No joke. Just a couple of idiots." I smiled at Bob, who was clearly ignorant of his son's past transgressions.

I shot Jackson a look, daring him to say more. His smile grew wider, but he remained silent.

Satisfied, I gave a final nod. "I'll see you later then."

"Morning, Becky." Pushing the kitchen doors wide, I grabbed an apron off the hook and strapped it around me, ready to work. "What's today's assignment?"

The scent of blueberries filled the air as Becky pulled a fresh batch of muffins from the rack oven that lined the back wall. She set them to cool on the expansive stainless steel island.

"Oh, Yeardley, am I happy to see you. We really need your help today."

"Sure. Where do you want me to start?"

"Right now, in the kitchen, but do you mind pinch hitting for Bob later? He's got a doctor's appointment this afternoon. I'm going to drive him," she explained.

"No problem." I worried, "Is he okay?"

Hearing my concern, she wrapped a reassuring arm around me. "He's fine. Just a few sun spots that need tending to. That's all." She squeezed me in a gentle hug. "It happens sometimes when you get to be our age and have spent your life enjoying the sun."

With a light touch, she tested the cooling muffins, arranging them neatly on large metal serving trays.

"While we're at the doctor's we could use your help tending to things out front. Monitoring the registers. Keeping an eye on the nursery. That sort of thing."

"What about Jackson? Isn't that his domain?"

"When he's not busy in the office or running pickups. It's too much for one person to manage alone. I know he'll appreciate your help."

"But, Becky, I haven't worked here in years. I don't have a clue what to do."

"I doubt that, honey." She hugged me again, thanking me. "It's like riding a bike. Once you learn, you never forget. And if you do, just ask Jackson."

The morning flew by as Becky and I worked in tandem to supply the bakery; Becky baking up a storm as I rushed about stocking and re-stocking all the baked goods. They disappeared almost as quickly as I put them out.

I had barely caught my breath before it was noon. A ravenous lunch crowd began to gather. Trading biscuits for Italian pie, I started hustling rounds of white and wheat dough to the crew working the outdoor pizza stand, keeping a watchful eye on their supply of toppings. When provisions ran low, I brought a fresh reserve.

"This is unbelievable." From the relative calm and safety of the kitchen, I peered through the porthole windows in awe. "Does it ever slow down?"

"November, usually. Once summer's over and the leaf peepers have come and gone."

Becky laughed at my dismay. "Trust me, it's a good thing. It keeps us warm and cozy in the winter."

I could see why. Greene's Market was booming. Filled with customers wanting, needing, demanding; brimming with products and produce from multiple vendors and farmers. Clearly, Jackson and his parents had the whole supply and demand thing pretty well figured out. Throw in a little creative ingenuity and some innovative thinking, and you had a one-of-a-kind shopping experience.

They made it look so easy, never letting on how much hard work and dedication went on behind the scenes. A lump formed in my throat as I thought about the past few days, and my temporary membership to this exclusive team. Time was flying way too fast.

"Isn't it time for you to go?" I asked, checking my watch. "Bob hates to be late for anything, even the doctor."

"You're right," Becky agreed.

Removing her apron, she hung it on its hook and stood in front of me. She took my hands in hers. "Now don't worry. You've got this. There's nothing you can't handle. If there is, ask Jackson."

Smiling with newfound confidence, I agreed. "I'm not worried. Everything will be fine. I promise. Take your time and do what you need to do. Jackson and I will close up tonight."

They drove away, Becky giving me the thumbs up as they pulled out of the parking lot. Once they were out of sight, I turned my attention to the business behind me, on the look out for my first call to action.

From this vantage, I could see the gift shop with its displays of sparkling jewelry, tapestry handbags, and cookbooks laden with recipes from local authors; wall plaques with hand-painted sayings like "What Happens at the Lake Stays at the Lake" dangled above drawers filled with decorative bottle stoppers, cookie cutters in all shapes and sizes, and more.

This nook of charming surprises and hidden treasures was new since my long ago days here. It was one of Jackson's additions to the already eclectic world of Greene's Market, and it was a gem. But right now, it looked like a hurricane had ripped through it. I had found my first project.

Completing one task then another, I made my way gradually through the store, tending to details that kept the train running smoothly on its track. The nursery, though well stocked, needed some TLC, so I returned plants, carelessly discarded and misplaced, to their proper spots. After that, I spritzed the rose bushes and watered the potted herbs.

I inventoried the cheese cooler, making notes of low quantities and popular selections, and put sample trays out to promote the cheeses we had in abundance. Like a wraith, I moved through the aisles, deftly dodging strollers and small children to answer their parents' questions; what's the difference between a

Big Boy and an Heirloom tomato? When will peaches be in? Do you carry Ben & Jerry's ice cream? Where are the bathrooms?

One of the cashiers waved to me, signaling for more $1 bills. I made a beeline for the office, grateful for the momentary escape. Much as I loved the chaos, solitude was an oasis worth visiting once in a while.

Jackson was sitting at his desk and hung up the phone as I entered. "Hey, how's it going out there?"

Looking every inch the CEO in jeans and a polo shirt, he relaxed into his high back leather chair and smiled, waiting for my report.

"No complaints. Customers are happy. Business is hopping. Register 3 needs ones."

"That's great." Reaching into the bottom drawer, he pulled out the petty cash box and started counting out bills.

"Thanks for helping out today, by the way. My folks really appreciate it." He handed me the money. "So do I."

Acknowledging his thanks with a smile, I grasped the packet of money, ready to go. Jackson held onto it like a tug of war, his green eyes piercing, a small smile flirting with the corners of his mouth. I swallowed, my lips parting slightly so I could breathe.

"Are you having fun?" he asked. Taken aback, I stopped to consider the question.

Becky was right. It was just like riding a bike. The familiar feel of the handlebars gripped firmly in my hands, legs pumping in circles, simultaneously balancing and moving me forward. It was thrilling, exciting and effortless. Like second nature. Like I had never left.

I had to admit, "I am. I really am."

Jackson let go of the money. I waved it like a fan in front of him.

"I better get this to the register. Can't keep the customers waiting for their change."

Jackson checked his watch and agreed. "It's almost closing time. I'll start locking up soon. Leave the registers open though until the last person's happily out the door. I'll take you home after."

"Well, that's the last of it." Jackson spun the combination lock, securing the cash drawers in the safe overnight. "Another day done, another dollar earned."

I snorted. "A tad more than a dollar, I'd say. This place is a goldmine."

Jackson nodded slightly. "Now it is. It was touch and go for a while there."

"What? Greene's is a staple, a landmark, a tradition." I searched for the words to aptly describe it. "How could it ever be anything less?"

Jackson did not answer right away. Tucking his hand under my elbow, he escorted me from the office, locking the door behind him.

"Come on, let's relax a minute." He winked mischievously.

Pulling a couple of beers from the store cooler, he walked me out to the patio and relaxed into the two-seater log swing. Using his key chain, he popped the caps from the bottles.

"Have a seat." He patted the space next to him. "It's been a long day. We've earned this."

We clinked bottles and drank, melting into the swing, letting our tired muscles relax from the hectic day. The swing swayed gently, rhythmically moving back and forth. A comfortable silence enveloped us.

A thought ran through my mind, jerking my eyes suddenly open. "Did you really almost close the market?" The thought was inconceivable to me.

Running a hand through his hair, Jackson stretched one arm across the swing behind me, as if to push the memory away.

"Not exactly. A few years ago, a super Woodmans' opened a few miles from here. You know those stores are like grocery palaces. It didn't take long before a lot of our customers started to drift over there, like kids to a candy store. The way I saw it, we could either close our doors or redefine who we are, what makes us special, different."

"Let me guess. You chose to go head-to-head with Woodmans'." I smiled and shook my head. Crazy.

"Hey, it worked for David. If he could battle Goliath, I could take on Woodmans'. Easy." We clinked again, taking long sips of our beers.

"Well, it worked," I complimented him. "What you've done with the place is incredible, and I don't just mean the money making part. It's really wonderful."

"Greene's Market: where tradition and convenience meet."

Genius. And true. By marrying long-standing traditions of dependable quality and service with modern technology and products, Jackson had created the ultimate consumer experience not found at any regular supermarket.

"Sort of like dusting off an old favorite and making it new again," I mused, turning to look at him.

Jackson was staring at me, or more precisely, my lips. My cheeks flushed and my skin grew warm. An invisible tug pulled me towards him. He lowered his head, bringing us face-to-face. I bit my lip, not sure where to look.

"Yeardley." Jackson whispered my name so softly, I was not sure he had spoken at all. He pressed his finger softly under my chin, raising my gaze to his.

"We were good together, weren't we? Back then."

Swallowing was hard, hearing even harder as the blood roared in my head. How many times had I dreamed of this moment? Of Jackson, my first love, my heartbreak.

As teenagers on the brink of adulthood, we had had no real cares or responsibilities, except each other. Nothing was more important to me than Jackson Greene. But that was then. We were different people now.

Jackson looked like a little kid holding his breath, waiting for me to answer. But he was not a boy anymore. I studied him intently, noting the masculine stubble on his cheeks, the faint lines etched into the corners of his eyes. The first signs of aging. I must look different, too. Older than the girl he remembered, but deep inside, still the same. Was he? A familiar ache pinched my heart. I missed my friend. I missed Jackson.

Jackson's expression was pained as if he felt it, too. Leaning back ever so slightly, he scanned my face, searching for something.

"I've never known anyone else like you, you know. I used to call you my Yeardley stick. I measured every girl I dated against you."

I sat in stunned silence. Unfazed, Jackson took a deep breath and pointed towards the store.

"The past few years, this place has been my girlfriend. My life really." Sensing my sympathy, he waved it off. "It's okay. It's what I wanted; to breathe new life into the business. Make it number one again. I wanted to make my parents proud."

"I'd say you've done that and then some."

"I have, haven't I?" Jackson chuckled softly, sounding as surprised as he looked. "Thank God."

"And give yourself a big pat on the back, too. You've done an amazing job here, Jackson. Cliché or no, this place runs like a well-oiled machine."

"Pretty much," he agreed, returning the compliment. "You're not too shabby either. You looked really happy working the floor today." He stared hard, as if daring me to deny it.

"You're right. I am happy. Working with Becky and Bob. Seeing so many familiar faces. Helping out where I can. I really missed it."

"And what about me? Have you missed me, too?"

Jackson's face was close to mine, his breath warm on my cheek. Pressing his lips to mine, he coaxed them to respond. They needed no encouragement. I kissed him back, making up for all the time we had missed.

Somewhere nearby, a throat cleared followed by a pronouncement. "Nola said you'd be here."

Ruth's words splashed over us like ice water, forcing us apart. She wore a good-natured smirk on her face. "Just like old times, I see."

"Ruth! You made it!" I jumped up and hugged her, grabbing the chance to hide my flushed cheeks and swollen lips from view. "I'm so excited you're here."

Breaking my grip, Ruth held me at arm's length. I squirmed under her curious scrutiny.

"Really? That's your story? That's not what it looked like to me." Laughing, she nodded at a sheepish Jackson. "Hey, Jackson. How's it going?"

"Ruth." Jackson nodded, suddenly without words. Raising the bottle to his lips, he took a long, cool sip of beer.

Ruth grinned, pulling me close for another hug. "I'm excited to see you too. God, it's been forever."

"We've got a lot of catching up to do," I agreed. "Did you just get here?"

With a shake that made her red curls bounce, Ruth explained, "I stopped by my folks place first, to drop off my stuff and say hello. Then I drove to Nola's but you weren't there. Obviously."

She looked meaningfully at Jackson and me.

Ignoring her, I asked, "Are the kids with you, your husband? I'd love to meet them."

Again, she shook her head no, casually wrapping her arm around my shoulders. "No way, girlfriend. I haven't seen you in years. This visit you're all mine. I'll introduce you to the family next time."

I liked the way she said 'next time,' like there was no doubt, I would be back again. I glanced at Jackson, his green gaze dazzling in return. The question was, how was I ever going to leave?

"C'mon," Ruth tugged at my hand, leading me towards her car. "Sorry, Jackson," she waved at him, never turning around. "I'm stealing Yeardley for a while. Cook out at my parents' house. You're welcome to stop by."

Glancing over my shoulder, I saw Jackson wave good-by. My heart skipped a beat, missing him already.

I waved good-bye and jumped into Ruth's car. "Let's go," I said, giving her the all set.

In a very unmotherlike fashion, Ruth peeled out of the parking lot. The tires squealed on the pavement as she pinned me with a fierce look. I braced myself for the inevitable.

"Girl, you better start talking!"

SHELBY

Riding in the back seat of Nola's car, I closed my eyes. A summer breeze flowed through the open window, clearing my mind as Lily's bright chatter soothed my worried soul. A frown formed before I could stop it. My eyes snapped open, alert but wary. When had I become such a worrier?

From the rearview mirror, Nola watched me, concerned. I felt a painful stab of guilt. This was her special week and I was ruining it. *Get over yourself, Shelby. Forget about Matt and California for a minute. Focus on the here and now.* Rolling my eyes, I smiled into the rearview mirror, and pointed to Lily. Chatting animatedly, Lily seemed oblivious to the nervous tension rolling off me in waves.

"Careful, Lily, or you'll be all talked out before we even get there."

An unladylike snort floated back to me. "Not a problem. I can talk enough for both of us."

Maybe I should have her talk to Matt for me, too. Ever since our 'sisters talk,' it was all I could think about: how selfish I had been with Matt. In my defense, being professionally courted by a top national firm was an incredible accomplishment. But Lily was right; Matt was my partner. He had a stake in this, too.

First thing this morning I had called him. The aromas of coffee and bacon wafting into the room made my stomach rumble, but breakfast would have to wait. This was way more important. Matt picked up on the second ring.

"Hey, babe, how are you?" Matt's voice crackled in my ear as the sound of the subway screeching down the tracks roared in the background.

"Hi, Matt. Guess I caught you on your way to work."

Matt looked around, a sea of blank faces looked back at him. Commuters on autopilot were gearing up for another day of work. The subway car jerked right, rounding a bend in the track. Matt hung tight to the steel pole in the middle of the car.

"Yeah, just me and my peeps. It's a real office party." Matt laughed at his own joke.

I smiled. Mr. Sunshine. He always made the best of every situation. "Hey, Matt, I just want to apologize. I've been so crazy with this California thing and what it means for me. But I know that it's not just about me. We're a team, you and me, and we're going to figure this out together, okay?"

Matt didn't answer. "Matt, did you hear me? I said I don't want to decide anything without you."

"Shelby?" Matt's voice was faint beneath the booming bass of heavy static. "Shel, I can't hear you. We're in a tunnel. Call me later."

My phone went dark as Matt ended the call. So much for setting the record straight. After breakfast, I tried to reach him again. When he didn't answer his cell phone, I called the receptionist.

"Hi, Shelby, how's your vacation going?" Cindy asked brightly. "I'm afraid Matt's in a meeting right now. Do you want me to have him call you when he gets out?"

I gave Cindy the cottage phone number. Cell service was notoriously erratic around here and I wasn't taking any chances. Matt needed to know I wasn't going anywhere without him.

As the time neared for the Donovan's barbecue, I still hadn't heard back from Matt. It was totally unlike him, and it was making me uneasy. Determined to reach him, I called him one more time. Matt's voicemail answered. "Hi, this is Matt. Please leave a message..."

Frustrated, I threw my phone in my purse. This was totally unacceptable. I needed to talk to Matt, and I needed to talk to him soon. Breathing deeply, I made a new plan as Nola drove us to the Donovan's. The minute we got back from the barbecue, I would call Matt. I didn't care what time it was. This was important. Feeling better, I leaned forward, tapping my sister on the shoulder. "Showtime, Lily."

Cars were already filling the Donovans' driveway when we got there, more pulled in behind us as we parked.

"Looks like a party," I mused.

I spotted Yeardley and Ruth carrying platters of food from the house to a long row of picnic tables, stretched end-to-end. Red and white-checkered tablecloths spread over them, like giant flapping wings weighed down by obscene amounts of food and jars of fresh cut daisies. Just like old times.

Weekly barbecues were a long-standing tradition with Nola and her friends. They enjoyed these regular gatherings as much for the food as for the chance to catch up. During the seasonal invasion of vacationing residents, the weekly barbecues were a quiet respite from the noisy business of summer.

My sisters and I had never questioned *if* there would be a cookout, just when and where, since everyone took turns hosting and grilling. The rest brought side dishes, desserts, and drinks. Nola always brought her 'famous potato salad' because somewhere in the Shepardsville bylaws, it is mandated that Nola's potato salad must be present at every social function.

Fortunately for all of us, she never seems to tire of making her special blend of bite-size potatoes, finely diced eggs, lots of chives for a little kick, and just enough mayonnaise to bind all the flavors together. Plus, a secret ingredient she swears she is either taking to the grave, or sharing with the first of her nieces to get married. It better be me.

Nola closed the trunk, the chilled salad bowl secure in the crook of her arm. "Ready, girls? You know everyone here. They're all dying to see you, so make sure you don't forget to eat while they're busy talking your ears off."

Lily and I nodded like the dutiful little girls we once were. "Yes, Aunt Nola."

With a smile she touched our cheeks. "I can't tell you how happy I am to have you both here. It's just like old times, isn't it?"

A couple of hours in, after gabbing and eating and gabbing and eating some more, I rolled myself off to a quiet corner where I could take it all in, unobserved. Everything was so familiar; the faces, the flavors, the harmonized chorus of voices talking and laughing. Like no time at all had passed. But it was different, too. For one thing, everyone was older. Nola and her crew were the new elders, while my generation had stepped into their shoes. A new posse of little ones ran around chasing fireflies in our stead. Like a game, everyone had advanced one square.

Lily's laugh tinkled through the air like wind chimes in a breeze. She had surrendered herself to the temptations of the dessert table, and was having fun mixing pies and puddings and pastries into the ultimate plate of treats. That was ironic. Lily had sworn off sweets years ago. Her body was a temple, respected and free from sin, except at the lake. Here it seemed even Lily could not resist the lure of the sweet smorgasbord. I watched in amazement, trying not to laugh as Lily circled the table in search of seconds.

Nola and Yeardley were nearby also, talking quietly and sipping white wine from clear plastic cups. In the setting sun, they glowed like shiny precious metals, Nola copper and Yeardley gold. They reminded me of my mom and Nola. Like my sisters and me, Natalie and Nola shared slight builds and delicate features, but the similarities between them ended there. Physically, Nola wore the porcelain skin of a redhead with a passionate temperament to match, while Mom's steady calm juxtaposed against her changing skin tone, from pale amber in winter to toasted marshmallow in the summer. Nola was deeply rooted in Shepardsville, more than content to stay on in her childhood home. Mom, like Lily, had bolted at the first opportunity with barely a backward glance. Similar but different in so many ways, they were just like Yeardley, Lily, and me.

Still deep in conversation, Yeardley was leaning against a tree, her spine pressed firmly against it for support. She looked young and slightly uncomfortable as she spoke to Nola, alternately blushing and laughing, and twisting her foot nervously in the dirt. If I didn't know better, I would say she was confessing something, but that didn't make sense. What could she possibly be guilty of?

The food for Nola's party! Panic gripped me as I scanned the crowd frantically looking for Becky. If there was a problem with the food, she would know about it. Skipping from table to table, I let my gaze roam out to the lawn where pods of people were catching up on news and local gossip. No sign of Becky.

From his front porch, Mr. Donovan was conducting a wine tasting of his latest vintages, pacing like an expectant father while his friends sniffed, sipped and swished until he couldn't take it anymore.

"So, what do you think?" he barked, stepping away from the makeshift bar to join them, giving me a clear view of the porch. No Becky there either.

From the corner of my eye, I caught sight of Jackson sitting alone on a picnic bench. I wondered if he knew where his mother was. Seemingly deep in thought, Jackson's gaze was keenly focused in front of him. He did not see me coming.

"Hey, Jackson. How are you?"

He startled, a guilty flush spreading across his face. Jumping to his feet, Jackson gave me a hug. "Hey, Shelby. Good to see you."

I hugged him back, craning my neck to see what had captured his attention. A short distance away stood a London Plane tree, a fairly common sight around here though I had to admit, this one was exceptionally beautiful with its smoothly mottled bark and leafy umbrella-like branches. Still, I doubted it was the tree that had Jackson so completely captivated. A movement on the ground drew my gaze downward. Nola and

Yeardley were sharing a hug of their own. Throwing a sideways glance at Jackson, I understood immediately.

"You still like her, don't you?" The question slipped from my lips before I could stop it, but his answering silence spoke volumes. "She likes you, too." I smiled encouragingly.

"I think so."

I had to strain to hear him, his voice was so low and he smiled sadly. *What the hell?* "Where I come from, that's a good thing," I said. "Am I missing something?"

Jackson raised his head, throwing his full attention on me. I returned his gaze.

"I like her, a lot," he confessed, clearly not afraid to share his feelings with me. "I'm pretty sure she likes me too, but..."

Impatiently, I pressed, "But what?"

Jackson was quiet, once again looking off into the distance. "She looks a lot like your mom, doesn't she?"

Following his gaze, I watched as the object of his attention and Nola walked with arms linked, over to where Lily was busy creating at the dessert table. Yeardley's lithe form moved gracefully, her thick mane of sun-streaked hair swinging behind her with every step. Catching sight of Lily's confectionary tower, her eyes flew wide, exposing thickly lashed pools of amber. Husky laughter burst from her lips.

"Very much," I agreed, not sure where he was going with this. "Is that a problem?"

"I barely remember your mom, or dad either." He continued to speak, ignoring my question. "I tried not to be around when they came to take you all home because as far as I was concerned, you were home."

He looked at me quizzically. "Is Yeardley a lot like your mom, too?"

I thought about that for a minute. Obviously there was a little of my mother in all of us, we were her daughters after all. Her logic and reasoning reigned supreme in me. Lily embraced her poise and composure. Yeardley's innate ability to connect with people from all walks of life was a genetic trait passed down directly from Mom. But of the three of us, I was definitely the most like her; intensely focused, obsessive, maybe even a little anal in our commitment to reaching our goals. A successful career, a loving partner and family; Mom had it all. I wanted it all too.

"Yeardley's more like my dad," I answered finally. "And a little bit of Nola, too." I shrugged unable to explain it. "Mostly she's just Yeardley."

The middle sister. Sandwiched between me and Lily, she was the glue that bound us together when we fought or disagreed, the cushion we leaned on when we needed comfort and peace, and the rock that never budged even when Lily and I were ready to throw in the towel.

"She's the strongest person I know," I finished, surprising myself.

"Me too," he agreed. "But I don't think she sees it. And she doesn't have a clue the affect she has on other people. She just sees herself as aimless, without purpose. She's dead wrong."

My brow shot up in surprise. This was getting deep. Joining him on the bench, I smiled, nudging his shoulder with mine. "Sounds like you more than like her. So why the long face?"

"I'm afraid this isn't enough for her." He waved his hand at the scene around us. "It wasn't for your mother."

"But Yeardley's not my mom!"

"I'm afraid I'm not enough for her," he confessed.

I thought about Matt. He was everything to me. But was I enough for him? Would he drop everything to move to California with me? My eyes burned, filling with salty tears. I bit my lip to stop them from leaking out. This was no time to get emotional. I needed to be strong like Yeardley. I had to fight for what I wanted.

"It ain't over till it's over," I said channeling Matt's beloved Yogi Berra. "Tell her how you feel. Let her decide if it's enough. You'll never know if you don't."

I squeezed Jackson's shoulder, encouragement for both of us. He and I both had some work to do.

"Hey, Jackson, do you know where your mom is?"

LILY

Delicious! I moaned softly letting the morsel of pie melt on my tongue. Normally, I tried to avoid eating sweets, but here at the lake everything just tasted so good! Besides, I had been working overtime on Aunt Nola's party. I deserved to indulge a little. Checking to see if anyone was near, I devoured another piece, bigger than the last.

"Oh. My. God!" A few heads turned in my direction, but no one came over. I put the plate down and walked away.

It was all about self-control. I could easily have eaten the entire dessert table. Instead, I chose to run through my party checklist one more time. Nola's extravaganza was just a few days away. We had to be ready.

First up, fireworks. Nola always loved watching the July 4th fireworks. They were her favorite. Abiding by an age-old unwritten code, the lakeside cottages always took turns, timing their displays for all to enjoy and making the fun last longer. Fireworks would cap off Nola's birthday celebration, too.

Next up, guests. I had to hand it to Yeardley. Paul Revere could not have done a better job spreading the word, I only hoped we would have enough food. Yeardley assured me she had that under control as well. Or at least, Becky did.

The back pocket of my jean shorts began to vibrate. Ignoring it, I licked my dry lips, catching a stray pie crumb into the dark recesses of my mouth. Landing square on my tongue, it exploded with flavor. The vibration grew stronger, insistent. Reaching into my pocket, I pulled out my phone and sighed.

"Hi, Diego."

Keeping my voice low, I tried not to sound annoyed. This was the third time today he had called.

"Diego, love. What's the matter?"

"Lily, I can't find the order forms for Brett Mullins' living room furniture. He's called several times wondering why it's taking so long. I tried to tell him the furniture delivery is on schedule. He wants to know the exact date."

I rolled my eyes thankful Diego could not see me.

"Brett's file is on my desk. Everything you need to know is in there. The furniture will be delivered on the 19th. Not before, not after. Marina and Lisa will coordinate the delivery and organize the accessories."

I paused, giving Diego time to digest the information. "Brett's young, Diego, and anxious. This is his first home, and he doesn't know how to handle it. He needs a little hand holding, that's all."

"He's a grown man. I don't have time for hand holding." Diego's time was normally dedicated to a more mature clientele.

"Honestly, Lily, I don't know how you deal with these young celebrities. They are so unbelievably needy!"

It was true. "But at the end of the day, Diego, their money is just as green as your clients' money. Try not to judge."

Pacified, Diego changed tactics. "Lily, please come home. Miami isn't the same without you. Neither am I. Come home. We'll take our own vacation. Anywhere you want to go."

Diego did not understand. I was exactly where I wanted to be right now. Taking charge of Nola's party was giving me a restless feeling about Alverez Designs. I was going to have to seriously rethink my plans when I got back to Miami.

"I'll be home soon, Diego." Slipping the phone into my pocket, I went to get some more pie.

YEARDLEY

"Take a drive with me." Jackson's fingers laced snugly with mine, coaxing me to go with him. "There's something I want to show you."

The cookout was over. Most of the diners had left, save for a final few stragglers; Nola, Shelby, Lily and I among them. We had stayed behind to help the Donovans clean up. Jackson stayed too, putting the last of the tables back in the shed and covering the grill until the next barbecue. Satisfied our work was done, I looked around for Nola. She was walking towards me with a tray full of candles and flowers.

"Go," she said, waving me off with one hand, expertly balancing the tray with the other. "Your sisters and I will be leaving soon, too. We'll see you at home."

"Are you sure?" I asked, reluctant to leave her. Nola had seemed off the whole night; quiet and distracted. "I'll come home with you."

"Don't be silly." The flames from the candles made her eyes shine as her lips curved in a mysterious smile. "This handsome young man's waiting for you." Nola lifted a strand of hair from my cheek, whispering for my ears only, "What are *you* waiting for?"

Excellent question. I slid into the seat next to Jackson and asked, "So where are we going?" Not that it mattered. I was happy to go anywhere with him.

In the dark, his teeth gleamed white as he put the truck in gear and pulled away. "You'll see."

He drove in silence, leaving me alone with my imagination unleashed. We had barely spoken since the market, earlier today. Since he had kissed me, and I had kissed him back. A wistful sigh escaped me. If only Ruth hadn't shown up when she did.

From the radio, Justin Timberlake crooned to me, interrupting my reverie; something about sharing tomorrows and falling in love. The problem was, I didn't have many more tomorrows left here. Nola's party was just two days away and the situation with Jackson was unsettled, to say the least. I had to sort it out, soon, but it wasn't going to be easy.

I had tried to bring it up with him at the Donovans'. It was a party after all, and friends talk at parties. Even Jackson had to agree that we had been friends, once; more than friends, but what about now? What about the kiss?

My skin had started tingling before I even saw Jackson. Arriving at the cookout a short time after Ruth and me, I knew the minute he was there. Standing a few feet away, Jackson was talking to Rick Stone and his wife. She was holding one of Jackson's hands to her very pregnant belly. I watched him laugh and smile with his friends as I discreetly checked him out.

Wearing faded jeans that hugged the length of his legs with the easy fit of a favorite pair of pants, he looked good enough to eat. I licked my lips, drinking in the rest of him. His suntanned forearms, strong beneath a pair of rolled up shirt cuffs, were only a brief distraction as I jealously caught sight of the snug, cotton embrace of his navy blue button down. Eagerly, I started to make my way over to him.

"Yeardley!" Appearing from nowhere, Miss Jean planted herself firmly in front of me. "Yeardley, we need to talk. I thought I had the perfect flavor combination for Nola's cake, but now, I'm just not sure anymore."

Miss Jean's big brown eyes threatened to overflow with worried tears. She needed my help. With a wistful glance toward Jackson making his way over to the buffet table, I led Miss Jean to a table of our own to talk. Mr. and Mrs. Bogart, Suzy Reece, and the Hogan twins soon followed; stopping to say hello, and introduce me to their grandchildren, fiancé, and new puppy respectively. I stayed put, happily catching up with so many faces from my youth, all the while keeping one eye trained on Jackson.

Making his own rounds, Jackson was a social mayor moving from one group to the next. One minute, joking with the guys, the next, holding Mrs. Flanagan's octogenarian elbow as she made her unsteady way through the buffet line. Whether he was talking shop with his dad at the beer keg, or chatting up Lily at the dessert table, that guy got around; always, it seemed to me, just beyond my reach. But not out of sight. All night long, I had felt the steady heat of his emerald gaze fixed on me.

So with Nola's blessing, here I was, riding with Jackson, wondering where the road would take us.

"I'd forgotten how much fun those barbecues are," I said, hoping to engage him in conversation. He nodded slightly, and I tried again. "And man, the food. It was amazing, but I ate way too much." Rubbing my stomach for emphasis, I groaned, "I don't think it will ever be flat again."

Jackson's green eyes glowed, scorching a trail from my head to my feet.

"You're perfect," he said, shifting his attention back to the road in front of him.

I shivered, already missing the heat of his gaze. "Are we almost there?"

Jackson nodded, turning into a now familiar driveway.

"Your place?" I asked, not sure why I was surprised. Coming here after the market had become our secret routine for unwinding after a long day's work. With the barbecue, I had forgotten all about it.

"Jackson, I really can't go swimming now," I objected. "Something's up with Nola, and I need to find out what it is. I'm sorry, I really should go home."

Jackson appeared at my door, giddy as a kid going to the circus. "It'll just take a minute."

Impatiently, he brushed my hands aside, unclasping my seat belt. He lifted me out of the truck. "You won't regret it, promise."

His excitement was infectious as we raced hand-in-hand across the lawn into his house. Stopping briefly, Jackson squeezed my hand, and smiled encouragingly.

"Just like old times, sneaking around in the dark."

I laughed, agreeing with him. He dragged me confidently up the stairs. "This way." I followed him into his bedroom.

Brilliant moonlight lit up the room, showing me all of its contents. An old oak bureau with six deep drawers rested against one wall. Nearby, a closet left open in haste bared its contents for the rest of the room to see. The light colored walls were mostly bare save for a few panoramic shots of the lake and surrounding hillsides. Above us, a ceiling fan cast lazy, swirling shadows onto the bed beneath it. I swallowed, taking in the queen-size bed, wearing a navy and white patterned quilt, and two fluffy, white pillows.

"What do you think?" Jackson smirked at me with arched eyebrows.

"Seriously?" *The nerve of this guy.* "That's the best you can do?"

A look of confusion wiped the smirk from his face. I almost felt bad. Almost.

Sweeping his arm with flourish, Jackson forced me to see what I had missed before: a giant, spyglass of a window streaming moonbeams onto his bed, while outside, the lake sparkled with breathtaking clarity.

"I challenge you to do better."

Jackson's smug smirk was back, but I could not be mad at him. I moved closer to the window in awe. This room, this view, this lake; they were the most beautiful things I had ever seen. I wanted to stay forever.

"Is it always like this?"

He nodded. "Pretty much. Even when the moon's not full, I feel like I'm sleeping in a tree house. I never want to close my eyes."

The colossal moon hung low in the sky, so close I was sure I could touch it. This spectacle of nature was an excellent reason to sleep with at least one eye open.

"I can see why," I said, placing my hand on his chest. "Thank you for showing me this, Jackson. It's incredible."

Jackson's heart beat like a staccato drum. Our eyes met. My pulse raced to catch up to his. We needed to talk.

"Jackson..."

"Shh," he hushed, placing a finger against my lips. "Me first."

He sat on the bed, patting the space beside him. "Sit, please."

I joined him, ignoring the alarms going off in my head to keep away. Where Jackson was concerned, I had no will power. To be safe, I allowed some precautionary space between us.

"The first time I laid eyes on this place, I knew I had to have it," Jackson said, looking around the room with pride. "It's special."

I smiled, agreeing with him. "It really is."

"And it deserves to be treated that way." He paused. "And so do you, Yeardley."

He squeezed my hand, a light pinch that captured my full attention.

"You've got it wrong, you know." Jackson stared at our conjoined hands.

I stared at him, dumbfounded. "Excuse me?"

"You think I left you," he said, "but it was the other way around. Every summer, you left me behind. And nothing has changed. In a few days, you'll be gone, again, and I'll still be here, where I've always been."

Jackson stared out the window, his handsome profile like marble in the moonlight.

"I want time, Yeardley." His voice was a husky whisper, and he squeezed my hand again, tightly. "More time, with you. Don't go back to Boston just yet."

Neither of us moved, afraid perhaps of what would happen if we did. Would I wake up and find it had all just been a wonderful dream? I could not take that chance. Sliding towards him, I closed the gap between us. Jackson's jaw was clenched, forbidding him to say any more. It was my turn to speak.

I gathered my courage, afraid I would say too much, or possibly, not enough. Either way, I was making this harder than it needed to be. The truth was, I only had one thing to say to him.

"Jackson." Cupping his chin, I forced him to look at me. "I want more time with you, too. Very much."

In the dim light of the room, Jackson's eyes were polished emeralds. They bored into mine with mesmerizing intensity. He smiled; the crooked smile that never failed to melt me, and pulled me onto his lap. Wrapping my legs around his waist, I hugged him tight. Neither of us was going anywhere.

Jackson held me close, burying his face in my neck, caressing it softly with his warm tongue. I moaned, arching beneath his touch.

"Please, Jackson," I begged, bringing his lips to mine.

Jackson's lips hovered over mine, teasing. I almost tasted them before he stole them away.

"What?" I breathed, reaching for him, aching for his kiss.

"Promise me," he demanded, grasping my greedy hands firmly in his. "Promise, you'll give us chance."

I shivered, missing the warmth of his strong hands caressing my body. I would have said anything to bring them back. This was too easy.

"Promise."

"No matter what?"

"No matter what," I laughed, feeling like two kids making a secret pact. "Do you want to pinky swear on it too?"

Jackson chuckled, gliding his hands up my back, and kissing me; softly at first, then deeply, as he rolled us onto the bed.

"Oh!" Sandwiched together, we were poised on the edge of something new, yet familiar, too. I clung to Jackson, losing myself in his kisses, but afraid to let go entirely. As if he sensed my doubt, Jackson flexed his shoulders firmly beneath my fingertips. I held tight to their broad expanse. My life raft. No matter what, Jackson would save me.

Jackson pressed his hips to mine; his desire obvious.

"Pinky swears are for kids," he murmured, nuzzling my ear. "I know a better way to seal the deal."

Brown/Corliss

173

THURSDAY

Brown/Corliss

SHELBY

From the solitude of the dock, I lay flat on my stomach, my chin resting upon my hands, as I stared out at the lake. The quiet of the early morning was giving way to the sounds of the coming day. This was my favorite time of day at the lake. Closing my eyes, I listened. A family of ducks swam by, mother duck in the lead quacking commands to her ducklings in tow. Sea gulls cried overhead as they scanned the water below for signs of breakfast, and a loud flopping splash sounded nearby. I smiled to myself. The legendary Big Fish was awake, too.

Rolling onto my back, I sighed with contentment and melted into the dock. The sun's golden touch warmed me all over. If only I could stay like this forever. A small frown nestled between my brows as I concentrated on the day ahead of me. There was still plenty of work to be done for the party, but I had other plans too. Nola and I were going for a hike in the glen where the rock face waterfalls and lush treetop canopy would give us cool respite from the hot afternoon sun. That was something to look forward to.

Something else I was looking forward to was talking to Matt. I had called him several times after the barbecue. He hadn't answered any of my calls. Then just as I was about to give up and go to bed, he had finally sent me a text: *At Doyle's. Didn't hear the phone. Call you tomorrow.*

That would be today. I looked at my watch, 8:00 A.M. Matt should be on his way to work. He had really been burning the candle at both ends this week, working all day and partying at night.

"The guys and I have been having a little fun," he explained when I asked him about it one time. "I feel bad. I haven't touched any of those dinners you made for me. We've been going out every night. Drinking and eating around Brooklyn, or as we like to call it, Brew and Chew."

Matt had certainly given me something to chew on. Lily thought I had been insensitive charging ahead with my plans for California without consulting Matt. But Matt did not seem to mind. He was busy doing his own thing, and there was nothing wrong with that. I was the one who left him behind for a week long vacation with my sisters. Fair was fair.

I had no reason to be worried, but I was. I couldn't help it and I couldn't stop wondering if things were changing between Matt and me. Were we strong enough to stick together through this? Would we try for a long distance relationship? My heart sank at the thought. Long distance relationships rarely worked out.

I glanced at the clock on my phone, 8:30 A.M. Matt should be at the office by now. Pulling on the heavy glass doors leading into the lobby, he would stand aside to let the people behind him pass through first. Following the crowd, he would stride across the gray and white marble tile floor to the coffee cart where Joe, the attendant, would have a large iced coffee, black with a spit of milk, waiting for him.

On the twelfth floor, Matt would enter the ATech offices, stopping to wish Cindy at the reception desk a good morning before making his way to his own office down the hall. From his office, Matt could see the Statue of Liberty holding her torch of gold. With a salute to her and a sip of strong coffee, Matt would be ready to start his day. But first, he would call me.

I stared at my phone, a dark screen sprinkled with confetti-colored squares. Any second, they would all disappear as Matt's call came through and his name popped onto the screen instead. Any second now Matt would let me know I was crazy to be worried about us.

"Shelby," Nola called to me from the porch. "I'm packing a picnic lunch for us later. Would you like roast beef sandwiches or chicken salad? Lemonade or ice tea?"

I looked at my still silent phone. "I'll be there in a sec, Aunt Nola."

LILY

The bagel popped out of the toaster like Jack in the Box. I grabbed the two halves and placed them on a worn plate with a sunflower design. Nola's kitchen was the heart of this home and every item in it brought back childhood memories.

"Lilyberry, can you set the table for dinner? Shelby, you're in charge of shucking the corn. Yeardley, can you make some fresh iced tea?" Nola would instruct each of us at night as the sun began its descent over the lake's horizon.

"Aunt Nola, I want to shuck the corn!" I would whine. Shelby always got the good jobs.

"Sorry, Lilyberry," Nola would say stroking my hair. "You know that's Shelby's job and she's the oldest. She gets to pick first."

"Shelby always picks the job I want!"

Shelby would stick her tongue out at me when she knew Aunt Nola couldn't see her. Back then I wanted to scream at Shelby to go away. Now, as I spread cream cheese on my bagel, I smiled at what a brat I must have been.

Nola came into the kitchen from the front porch. "Are you sure you don't want to come with Shelby and me for a hike? We're going to have a picnic lunch near the waterfalls."

I rolled my eyes at Nola. "Sure," I said sarcastically. "There's nothing better than fresh air and exercise."

"You must be in the fresh air all the time in Florida. The weather is gorgeous there," Nola commented, ignoring my sarcasm.

"I am. But I can assure you there is no exercise involved. A good beach chair and the side of a pool is all I need."

"You girls have been running around all week working on my party. I would love to just spend a little quiet time with you and Shelby. It would be perfect if Yeardley was here too, but it seems she's a little preoccupied. How about if I promise we'll walk very slowly?" Nola asked as she put extra napkins in the picnic basket and grabbed a bottle of sunscreen from the kitchen counter.

I was not the least bit excited about hiking through the fields to the waterfalls, but I was sure Nola had packed a fabulous lunch and food was a big enticement for me this week. Diego would shake his head if he knew what I had packed away in the last few days.

"Okay," I said reluctantly. "But on one condition. We walk slowly and you put a bottle of wine in that picnic basket so we can celebrate when we reach the waterfalls."

"Done!" Nola said with a smile. "Now run and put on some comfortable shoes. And grab a hat; it's going to be sunny and hot by the time we get there. Shelby and I will meet you out front." She grabbed a bottle of wine from the rack and waved it in the air at me.

I ran upstairs to change; the thought of hiking in the summer heat and working up a sweat was not the least bit appealing. But Nola was right. I only had a few more days at the lake and I should be spending it with my family.

Fifteen minutes later, we looked like an abbreviated version of the von Trapp family singers, moving in a single line across the landscape. Of course, I was last in line, several paces behind Nola. Shelby led us with the enthusiasm of a young girl. No surprise there, she committed 100 percent to everything she did.

I purposely waited almost an hour before starting to whine. "Guys, do you think we can slow down a little bit? My legs are starting to seize up and I'm a little out of breath." I theatrically gasped for effect.

Shelby looked at her watch. "Forty-eight minutes!" she called loudly over her shoulder, not bothering to slow down. "It took forty-eight minutes for you to start complaining. Not bad! I told Aunt Nola it would be less than half an hour."

I tried to look insulted, but Shelby was right. Physical activity was not my strong suit. "Okay, okay. You don't have to be smug about it. I never claimed to be an athlete."

Nola slowed to a stop and called to Shelby, "Let's go a little further to Windy Falls and then we can set up a spot for lunch." Nola turned around and looked at me sympathetically. "Lily, honey, can you make another fifteen minutes or so?"

"I guess so," I pouted. "But we need to have a nice, long lunch so I can get my strength back." I tried my best to look pitiful.

"Deal!" Nola said with a smile and reached for my hand to pull me along the trail.

Windy Falls consisted of a fifteen-foot waterfall surrounded by pine and birch trees and grassy knolls. The waterfall was most active in early summer when the winter ice on the lake melted, forcing the water down the falls and eventually to a nearby river.

"Over here," Shelby called, spreading a small blanket on a grassy spot just a few feet from the water's edge. A canopy of trees provided a semblance of shade. I followed Nola over to Shelby and took the picnic basket from her hands.

"Let me do that for you, Aunt Nola," I offered. The basket was chock full of sandwiches and summer salads. Two containers held iced tea and lemonade and across the top of the basket was a lovely bottle of Pinot Grigio.

I pulled out the contents and spread them out on the blanket. Shelby passed out plates and utensils while Nola grabbed a corkscrew and went to work opening the bottle of wine.

"I normally don't drink this early in the day," I said, reaching for a wine glass, "but I need to celebrate the fact that I made it here. Anyone else?"

"Sure," Nola replied. "I'd like to celebrate that too. I am just so happy to spend some time with you girls. I know you lead very busy lives, but I've really missed you. Summer time was so magical here when you were younger." Nola's voice trailed off as she looked away towards the water.

"Aunt Nola, don't be sad," Shelby chimed in. "We were all anxious to get back here. Your invitation came at the perfect time. We miss you too."

We helped ourselves to chicken salad sandwiches, potato salad, blueberries, melon and homemade biscuits. I treasured every bite of Nola's decadent food and washed it down with a generous glass of wine.

Nola wiped biscuit crumbs from the edge of her mouth with a napkin. "Lily, tell me more about how things are going for you in Miami. I get bits and pieces from your mother. Are you happy there? How is your job going?"

I pushed the hair back from my face and twisted it into a bun, securing it with an elastic band. "I love Miami. I really do. The weather is great. The people are great, for the most part. I love being a designer. But..." I hesitated.

"But what?" Shelby asked, scooping melon onto a spoon and slurping it into her mouth.

"Well..." I thought about what I wanted to say. This week had been exhilarating, planning Aunt Nola's party. I loved having total control over everything; making my vision a reality.

"Aren't you in charge of your own designs in Miami?" Nola asked.

I thought carefully about the answer to that question. The short answer was 'yes,' but at the end of the day, it was still Diego who had the final say. Most of the time he saw things my way, but when he didn't, I would have to defer to my superior; even when it went against my better judgment. Nothing made me angrier.

"For the most part, Aunt Nola. Diego pretty much lets me do my own thing. But when we butt heads, it can be so frustrating. I've been thinking all week that maybe I need a change. Something that allows me to call my own shots."

Nola smiled. I thought I caught a little sadness in her eyes. "Princess Lily, you have so much talent. You've been creating masterpieces since you were five years old."

"Exactly," I agreed. "Imagine what I could do if I was the captain of my own ship?"

"I have no doubt that you would be wildly successful with your own firm. But remember, you would be all alone. You and Diego have each other to rely on for support and inspiration. Take it from me, being by yourself sometimes gets lonely." Nola picked up the leftovers and began to wrap them in foil.

Shelby chimed in, "Yeah, Lily. Didn't you tell me a few days ago that I needed to make big decisions as a team? Are you really ready to say goodbye to your partnership with Diego?"

I hesitated. "You know, I love Diego. I have no idea if we'll be together forever. I can't think that far ahead! He is a good man, I'll give him that. I just want a little more freedom. But I'm not sure he wants to give me any more authority."

"I'm going to tell you exactly what you told me. Talk to him about it, Lily. Tell him how you really feel and see what happens. You can't make up his mind for him, you know," Shelby said, sipping on a glass of iced tea.

"Excellent advice," Nola said with a wink. "Lily, you'll be successful no matter where you go. Wouldn't it be more fun to have someone who loves and supports you by your side?"

I appreciated that Shelby and Aunt Nola understood my discontent. My colleagues would never give me any encouragement. They were too busy with their snarky comments about me and Diego. Carolina was probably right, they were just jealous.

"I know. I know. I will talk to him when I get back to Miami. He's just going to have to understand that I need something more if we stay together. But you're both right. He can't help me if I don't tell him what's bothering me." I drained the last sip of wine from my glass. "Thanks, guys. I love you both. I really do."

Shelby started gathering up the picnic blanket. "Okay you two, we should head back before Princess Lily turns into a pumpkin."

Nola stood and faced the water, a serene look on her face. "Today has been perfect." She turned back towards us. "Thank you. I will treasure this day for a long time."

FRIDAY

Brown/Corliss

189

NOLA

Nola opened her eyes and stared at the clock. It was 8:30; time to get up and start breakfast. When the girls were teenagers, they used to sleep until noon. It would drive Nola crazy. They were wasting so much of the day. But today, she understood the joy of stealing a few extra minutes in bed.

You're stalling, said the voice in her head. Nola ignored it, reflecting instead on Wednesday's barbecue. Watching the girls mix and mingle with their old friends had been fun. It was clear to Nola that they belonged here. Like Nola, they had become part of an extraordinary extended family steeped in friendship and love. It made what she had to tell her nieces this morning even harder. Reluctantly, Nola pushed herself out of bed.

It took only a few minutes to throw on a robe and brush her teeth. Nola headed for the kitchen. This morning she would make blueberry pancakes, the girls' favorite. It would start the day on a good note, before she told them the news. Nola sighed, afraid of how the girls would react. Yeardley would be the most emotional. She would instantly recognize the severity of the situation. Shelby would digest the news, taking time to sift through all the pieces and sort them out. Lily was the wildcard. Nola could imagine a few different reactions, none of them good.

By 9:00, the aroma of pancakes and coffee was wafting towards the stairs. Predictably, Shelby was the first one down.

"You are NOT making pancakes, are you?" Grabbing an empty mug from the cupboard, Shelby poured herself a cup of coffee.

"I am," Nola replied, concentrating on the griddle in front of her. "Have a seat. The first batch should be ready in a minute. How are you? Were you able to connect with Matt last night?"

A shadow passed over Shelby's face. "You know, Aunt Nola, I'm trying not to let Matt distract me. It's almost your birthday. I just want to focus on that and enjoy my time here with you."

"You know, you girls really don't have to make such a fuss about my birthday! Having the three of you here this week has been present enough." Nola waved her spatula at Shelby. "A store-bought cake and hamburgers on the grill would have been fine by me."

"I know. I know," Shelby replied. "It's been fun though, and really nice seeing everyone again. You're so lucky to have this place, Aunt Nola. It's a little slice of heaven."

Nola felt the pain in her chest return. "Breakfast is ready," she said. "Why don't you go call your sisters?"

"Leave some for the rest of us, would you?" Yeardley complained as Lily stacked a tower of pancakes onto her plate.

"Don't worry, Nola's made plenty." Lily smiled sweetly at her sister. "Pass the syrup, please."

Chewing on a strip of bacon, Shelby watched them, amused. "Orange juice?" she offered, filling their glasses. "How about you, Aunt Nola?"

Nola stared into her coffee cup, lost in thought.

"Aunt Nola, is everything okay? You haven't touched your breakfast. It's going to get cold."

Her concentration broken, Nola smiled warmly at Shelby. "I'm fine." Pushing her plate aside she said, "I need to talk to you girls about something."

Nola folded her hands on the table in front of her. "There's a reason I asked you all to return to the lake. For my birthday, of course, but there's something else."

The girls exchanged looks. "What is it, Aunt Nola?" asked Shelby speaking for the group.

Nola had been dreading this moment all week. "There's no easy way to say this. I think the best thing is to start at the beginning."

"A few months ago, I received a phone call from a man named Steven Fontaine. He said that several of my friends had suggested he contact me. They had all signed onto a business proposal and thought I might be interested in hearing about it as well. He listed their names: the Greenes, the Burkes, the Rollins and the McGuires. His proposal concerned an initiative to bring sustainable energy to the lake."

"Great idea," Yeardley agreed.

"I thought so, too."

Nola continued. "Mr. Fontaine seemed very knowledgeable. He spent several hours here, showing me his plans and telling me about his project. The basic idea was to build wind and solar power structures that work in conjunction with Mother Nature to provide natural energy to the lake community. The benefits included enhanced service for year-round residents and a return on investment for providing the energy source to summer residents and businesses. He had pamphlet after pamphlet of environmental studies, energy studies, state and town approvals, and expected investments profits.

Nola's throat was dry. She took a sip of her coffee.

"Mr. Fontaine had only a few investment spots left. He explained that each investor became an automatic shareholder of the company. Once all the systems were in place, profits would be shared with the investors in a quarterly dividend."

It had seemed idiot proof. Lake residents, who were also investors, would benefit two-fold; from enhanced energy service and a dividend bonus.

"It was the opportunity of a lifetime, to get in on technology at its inception. It all seemed so exciting. Construction of the energy infrastructure would begin this summer. He left me all of the paperwork and told me I had a little time to make up my mind. I read through the information and made a list of questions. Mr. Fontaine answered them all, without hesitation. I called Becky Greene to see how she and Bob felt about making the investment, but she was still at the market. I never actually talked to her. "

Nola paused, rubbing her hands together. They felt cold.

"I was so certain about this opportunity. It was a chance for me to be a part of something big, something important to Shepardsville. It would be my way of making a difference, much like your grandfather and great-grandfather had done. The investment buy-in was a lot of money, but I knew it would be worth it."

The table was quiet. After a moment, Yeardley broke the silence.

"You make a difference every day, Aunt Nola. Everything you do seems to be for someone else's benefit."

Speaking to her aunt, Yeardley looked sideways at her sister. "Shelby, too. You're both so busy doing, you don't see the effect you have on everyone around you."

Nola squeezed Yeardley's hand and tried hard not to cry.

"When I couldn't reach Becky, I decided to do a little research of my own online." Nola continued in a strained voice. "Mr. Fontaine had a website that pretty much summarized everything he told me. There were testimonials from other investors and website links to the technology that he planned to bring to the lake. It was professional and contained the same contact information that was on the pamphlets. I was satisfied with what I saw."

"A few days after I had signed the papers and given him my check, I had a few more questions. I called his cell phone and got his voice mail. I tried several more times over the next few days, but he never answered. By the fourth day, the phone number was disconnected. I drove to Grandton to the address on his business card. It wasn't an office at all. It was a coffee shop."

Nola felt sick all over again.

"I went home and called my friends who had also invested. I wanted to warn them."

"What did they say?" Lily asked her eyes wide.

"Oh, girls, they had never heard of him! Not one of them knew who he was." Nola could not hold back any longer. She began to sob uncontrollably.

Shelby reached to comfort her.

"It's okay, Aunt Nola. I'm sure we can fix this, somehow. How much money did you give Mr. Fontaine?"

Nola lifted her head. Tears streamed down her cheeks.

"I gave him everything. The buy-in amount was more money than I had in cash. I went to the bank and Conrad Hopper helped me fill out the paperwork for a home equity loan. The cottage has been paid off for decades so its value is all equity."

"Didn't Mr. Hopper ask you what it was for?" Shelby asked, stroking Nola's arm.

"No. He really couldn't for privacy reasons. But you don't know how much I wish he had. Maybe he would have talked me out of such a stupid, stupid decision."

Nola stood, pushing her chair away from the table.

"By the time I realized that I had been duped, Mr. Fontaine had cashed my check and disappeared. It's all gone, every bit of it. That includes the house. There's no money to pay back the loan."

Shocking the girls into silence, Nola hurried from the room.

YEARDLEY

"It's done," said Nola. "I told the girls."

Passing by Nola's bedroom, the door slightly ajar, I stopped to listen. She whispered into the phone.

"Not well," she said, answering a question I could not hear but could easily assume. "Especially Yeardley. I'm really worried about her."

Nola continued, murmuring softly into the phone. I marveled at her gentle selflessness in the face of such horrible news. Losing the cottage was inconceivable. I was barely coping myself. How was Nola ever going to survive such a devastating loss? I wondered if I should stay and console her, or slip away, unnoticed.

A harsh bark, barely recognizable as laughter, blasted suddenly through the cracked door, obliterating any thoughts I had of leaving.

"I don't have a choice, Jackson," Nola said. "The cottage is yours."

At the sound of his name, I froze in place. What did Jackson have to do with this? I inched closer to the door, hoping for some insight.

A large canopy bed rested prominently in the center of Nola's room. It was one of many Hamilton family heirlooms that filled the cottage, but this one was special. It was Nola's favorite. I spotted her immediately, perched beneath the billowy canopy like a wounded bird in its nest. She had aged instantly it seemed; the fine lines of her face settling into deep furrows of worry. Even her once-perfect posture had crumbled, surrendering to an invisible pressure that forced her chest down to her knees. I hardly recognized her, this sad imposter of the fearless aunt we had long ago crowned, Nola the Fierce.

We called it the Medieval Summer, when our imaginations had been fueled by Nola's incredible stories of fire-breathing dragons, and castle moats filled with ferocious snapping creatures. She told us the Cottage Kingdom must be protected and defended at all costs. She taught us how to duel using our neon water noodles as swords, and we pranced around the lawn behind her, facing our enemies, head on. Nola challenged anyone who dared to cross her; the mighty lawn oak, the garden patch sunflowers, and anyone else who dared to trespass. No foe was too big for Nola the Fierce.

Nola's make believe was a great force, but her love was even stronger. That magical summer, my sisters and I learned that there was nothing that confidence and courage could not conquer, and that love was the most powerful weapon of all.

And just maybe I thought, the most dangerous. *I don't have a choice, Jackson.* Nola's accusation ran through my head, filling it with doubt. Nola had loved Jackson since the day he was born. Now he was breaking her heart.

Instinctively, I placed a hand over my own heart, cheered by its strong and steady beat, so far so good. Maybe I was wrong about Jackson. Maybe he wasn't the devil in disguise. Just the thought of him tickled goose bumps on my arms. At the same time, a strange sensation swept through me. Something was shattering deep inside. Thousands of tiny cracks were streaking across the unprotected chambers of my heart. My chest tightened, desperate for air, as my heart clenched in fear. This was not going to end well.

Outside Nola's door, I listened as her conversation with Jackson wrapped up. She prepared to sign off first.

"I'd like to wait until after the party," she said. "I don't want the girls to be here for that part of it. Can we put it off for a few days?"

My blood was boiling before she finished speaking. It was bad enough Jackson was taking the cottage, now he was making Nola grovel, too. I felt sick, but Nola seemed filled with gratitude.

"Thank you, Jackson," she said. "For understanding. I'll see you Saturday at the party."

199

I flew down the hall to my room, carefully avoiding the creaky spots that would tip Nola off to my eavesdropping, and flopped onto my bed. This was my sanctuary, my thinking room, where all of my best plans were made. Several large windows overlooked the lake, letting in the light and air for clear-headed thinking. The bed was not too soft or hard, but just the right support for a girl with a lot on her mind and an even heavier heart.

Jackson, what have you done? Worse still, what was I thinking, believing in him again? Believing the other night was a new beginning for us. *No matter what,* we had vowed to each other. But today was a different story. Jackson had broken his promise. I hated him.

Closing my eyes, I tried to think about everything that had happened. It was pretty clear. Nola was losing the cottage because of a stupid scam, and Jackson was taking complete advantage of her misfortune, scooping the place up, for himself. It was the first time I had ever known Nola to make a mistake, and this was a big one. I was certain that right now she was beating herself up for letting the family down. Nola considered herself the keeper of the Hamilton family legacy, and now it was lost, because of her. Trying to do the right thing, Nola had lost everything.

But Jackson was a different story. He had spent the past week charming his way back into my life, winning my heart, and earning my trust. But for what? If Nola's cottage was already his, what did he need me for? . The question plagued me until I couldn't take it anymore. If Jackson wanted more time with me, I was going to give it to him. Just enough to tell me exactly what the hell was going on.

When I arrived at Greene's, Jackson was stacking cellophane packages of buttermilk biscuits on one of the oversized fruit carts. White pastry nestled between tidy rows of shiny red strawberries, their green quart containers overflowing. He looked up, smiling as I approached.

"Whoa!" Jackson caught my hand before it collided with his cheek. "What the hell...?"

Momentarily blocked, I paused long enough to take aim with my other hand. Once again, Jackson caught it before it could hit its mark. Frustrated beyond belief, I glared at Jackson through my boiling rage. Still holding my hands firmly in his, Jackson pulled me out of the market and into the dim coolness of the stockroom.

Spinning on his heels, Jackson confronted me. "Yeardley, what the hell is going on?"

Jackson's eyes searched mine, demanding an explanation. But I couldn't speak. The words were stuck in my throat. I stared at him, mute, collecting my thoughts while Jackson stood in front of me, concerned but pissed. I doubted that he had almost been slapped by a girl before. Then again, I had never tried to slap anyone before either. This was a first for both of us.

"I could ask the same of you," I replied, finding my voice again. "I don't know what the hell kind of stunt you are trying to pull, but you're not going to get away with it. I won't let you."

In the silent storeroom, neither of us spoke, using the time to size up our opponent. Jackson was bigger than me but I could hold my own against him. I knew the truth. A chill crept over me as Jackson glared at me with reptilian eyes. His words pelted like hail stones.

"Do you mind telling me what this is all about, please? Or am I supposed to read your mind?"

"We both know why I'm here, Jackson. What I don't understand is, how could you?" My composure was starting to slip and tears pricked at my eyes.

Jackson looked away, hands on his hips, and shook his head. "Play fair, Yeardley," he said. "No tears."

"This isn't a game, Jackson!"

"Then what is it?" His face flushed with anger. "You storm in here like a raving lunatic, making no sense at all, and I'm supposed to figure it out? Is this about Nola? I would think you'd be happy."

The spotlight was on me now. Jackson waited, expectantly. *Was he crazy? What about this could possibly make me happy?* He had not confessed or explained, or even begged for my forgiveness. Clearly, I had underestimated him.

Jackson's eyes were clouded with anger and resentment. He wasn't budging and I was suddenly drained. It was over. Jackson and I were never going to work our way out of this no-win situation.

"Game over, Jackson," I surrendered with a warning. "Stay away from Nola. Stay away from my family. Stay away from me. I never want to see you again."

I ran out of the store and jumped into the Camry, eager to get away before the threatening storm hit. Pulling quickly out of the parking lot, I made it back to Nola's, just as the first teardrop fell.

SATURDAY

PARTY DAY

Nola pushed the hair back from her face and glanced at the clock. It was still early morning, but the sun was shining and motorboats were already purring on the lake. Today would be bittersweet. The girls had worked so hard to make this birthday unforgettable. Now, it truly would be. Nola pulled a pillow over her head. She didn't have the strength to get out of bed.

Surprising herself, Lily was the first one downstairs. The others must still be sleeping. Yesterday had been a dark day. Nola's news had thrown them all for a loop. Still, Lily was sure there was some way to make things right again. With a little time, she and her sisters could figure it out, but not today. They had to get through Nola's party first.

Lily made her way into the kitchen. What they all needed was a hearty breakfast to get the day started. She grabbed the coffee pot first. Caffeine was a priority. The aroma of percolating coffee filled the air as Lily inventoried the refrigerator.

"Where is everyone?" Shelby wandered into the kitchen, stopping short at the sight of Lily, her head buried in the refrigerator. "I thought you were Aunt Nola."

"No Aunt Nola this morning," Lily replied. "Not yet. I'm making breakfast today."

Shelby poured herself a cup of coffee, and stirred in cream and sugar.

"Do you think Aunt Nola is okay, Lily? It must have been so hard for her to tell us about the cottage."

"It's hard to believe that Aunt Nola would risk everything that way," Lily agreed. "I kind of understand it, though. Taking care of the family home has always been Aunt Nola's responsibility. It's her job. But just because she chose this life, it doesn't mean she can't want more. I totally get that."

Shelby was impressed. Once again, her baby sister was the voice of reason.

"You may be right," she agreed. "Let's wait until Mom and Dad get here. We'll fill them in on what's happened. Maybe they can help."

Lily smiled. "Sounds like a plan. But until then, we have one hell of a party to get ready for. At least for tonight, I want Aunt Nola to put her worries aside."

Shelby was already half way out the door. "I'll go wake Yeardley. We need her help."

Opening the door to Yeardley's bedroom a crack, Shelby popped her head inside. Yeardley was still in bed, the sheet pulled tight under her chin, wadded tissues littered across it like cotton balls. Shelby raised the window shades, letting the morning sun spill into the room.

"Yeardley." Shelby sat on the edge of the bed. "Yeardley, it's time to get up."

Yeardley stirred, tossing the tissues to the floor as she rolled to face her sister.

"What time is it?"

"Late." Exasperated, Shelby coaxed her out of bed. "Look, I know this business with Jackson is making you sick." Inconsolable was more like it. After Yeardley had sobbed the details of her encounter with Jackson to Shelby and Lily, Shelby had had no choice but to put her to bed.

Yeardley opened her mouth to speak but Shelby raised a hand to silence her. "If you're right about Jackson, I'm sick too, but we can't think about it right now. We have a party to put on. A party like no one has ever seen. We have to do it, for Nola. Everything else can wait until tomorrow."

Shelby's words sank in slowly. "I'll be right down," Yeardley said at last. "For Nola."

"For Nola," Shelby nodded. Closing the door behind her, she continued along the hallway to Nola's room.

The door to Nola's room was shut tight. Shelby pressed her ear against it, and listened closely. Nola's deep breathing was the only sound she heard. That was good. Nola needed her rest. Shelby tiptoed back to the kitchen.

"All set?" Lily asked as Shelby entered.

"Yes. Yeardley's on her way down, Nola is sleeping. If she's not up by the time Mom and Dad get here, I'll wake her."

"Perfect," said Lily. "That's easier than trying to work around her. I'd like to keep some things about tonight a surprise." She looked to Shelby for agreement.

Shelby rolled her eyes. "Relax, Lily, everything's going to be perfect. You have this party planned right down to the candles on the cake."

"The cake! Where's Yeardley?"

"Right here." Yeardley walked into the kitchen, stifling a yawn. "I need coffee."

Already a step ahead of her sister, Lily handed Yeardley a steaming cup. "Drink up, Yeardley, you have a million things to do today. First up, check on Miss Jean. Find out when the cake is going to be delivered."

"I live to serve." Yeardley forced a smile to her lips. "I'm on my way"

Lily was scanning the checklist in her hand. "Oh, and ask her if she has any ideas how to display the cake without it melting. If she doesn't, I'm sure I can figure something out."

Before Yeardley could respond, a car horn blared from the driveway, followed by a knock on the door.

"Hello? Anyone home? Anyone here turning 65 today?"

"Mom! Dad!" Yeardley ran to welcome her parents.

Natalie and Thomas greeted each of their daughters separately, stepping back for a full inspection.

"Looks like you've been having a great time at the lake," Thomas observed.

"Fresh air and lake water," said Natalie. "That's what keeps Nola looking so good." She looked around the room. "Where is the woman of the hour?"

Linking arms with her parents, Shelby spoke pointedly to her sisters.

"Lily, Yeardley, why don't you two do what you have to do. I'll show Mom and Dad their room and bring them up to speed."

With a kiss and a wave, the girls scattered like leaves on the wind.

Shelby smiled at her parents. "Come on. You haven't been here in a long time. Let's get you reacquainted with everything."

Standing on the shoreline, Natalie breathed deeply, memories of her childhood washing over her like the cool lake water.

"I do love it here," she said, turning to her husband. "We should visit more often."

It was the segue Shelby had been waiting for.

"Why don't we sit down for a minute." She gestured to a circle of nearby Adirondack chairs. "I want to talk to you about something."

"Honey, is everything okay? Matt? Your job?" Her father asked.

"No, no. It's not about me. It's about Aunt Nola."

After they were all seated in a close semi circle, Shelby continued.

"Nola shared some devastating news with us last night. Nola is in a bad way, and the three of us are pretty shaken, too. We don't know what to do."

Natalie leaned forward, taking Shelby's hand.

"What is it, Shelby?"

Taking a deep breath, Shelby told her parents the distressing details of what had happened. As she spoke, Natalie covered her mouth in disbelief. Thomas rubbed her back soothingly.

When Shelby had finished, Natalie looked out over the lake, speaking so quietly her daughter and husband had to lean close to hear her.

"Nola has always done the right thing," Natalie explained. "She looked after my parents when they were older. She's kept our family's home intact so we could all enjoy and share it. And she's done it all on her own."

Natalie's shoulders drooped. "I haven't been there for her like I should have been. I feel so ashamed."

She turned to look at her husband. "I need to make it up to Nola. I need to help her fix this, and make everything right again. Thomas, we can't leave until we do."

Thomas placed a comforting hand on his wife's shoulder. "We will. And we'll do it together."

Shelby hugged her parents in relief. "This is more than even I can handle. I knew you would help. We'll get to work on it in the morning. For now though, let's just make this a night that Nola will never forget."

PARTY TIME

It was almost five thirty. The party started at six o' clock sharp, and Lily was still in her shorts and a t-shirt. In a minute, she would go change into her cotton sundress. But first, one final check to make sure everything was in its place and ready to go.

Lily walked the perimeter of the yard, a huge grin splitting her face. It was all exactly as she had planned. Center stage on the front lawn stood a large white tent. It was lit from within by thousands of twinkling lights strung across the ceiling and streaming down the support poles. Sand bags filled with sparklers lined the outside of the tent, ready to be lit when Nola cut her birthday cake.

Inside the tent, summer blossomed with Mrs. Rollins' designer centerpieces of purple hydrangeas dressed in white lilacs and greens. On the tables, lilac linens and white china shared space with camp-style kerosene lanterns, and canoe-shaped shakers. Ribbon wrapped mason jars, filled with lemonade mix and two straws added a touch of festive fun to each place setting. Bearing a metal appliqué with '*Nola July 25, 2014,*' the party favors were a sentimental reminder of one very special person and an extraordinary celebration.

With a practiced eye, Lily surveyed the rest of the space. To one side, a white ruffled buffet table waited with chafing dishes steaming and ready to serve. Across the room, a large elegant bar stood fully stocked with champagne, wine and beer. There would be no shortage of food or beverages at this party.

It was the calm before the storm. As Frank Sinatra crooned, "I've Got the World On a String," Carson Andrews fine-tuned the sound system: background music for dining, rowdy energy for the dance floor. On the shoreline, Cam Brown was putting the finishing touches to a pyrotechnic spectacular that was sure to wow. Seeing Lily, Cam gave her two thumbs up. Everything was ready to go. All they needed now was guests.

Shelby approached from the house. "Lily, everything looks amazing! Very Retro Lake Chic."

Shelby spun around slowly, taking in the scene. "I have to admit, I had my doubts, but shame on me. Lily, you totally nailed it. You've captured the essence of the new and the old in one seamless, fabulous party!"

Lily grinned broadly. "Thanks, sis. It wasn't easy, but it sure was fun."

Seeing Shelby dressed in a beautiful light blue sundress and silver sandals, Lily remembered one last thing she had to do.

"I need to change before everyone gets here. Do you mind taking over for me?"

"Go ahead. I'll be here." Shelby waved her off. "And take your time. You've earned it."

A large silver truck rolled up the driveway. Craning her neck to see who it was, Shelby hurried to greet them.

"Oh my gosh, you guys!" Shelby hugged Becky, Bob, and Jackson individually. "You've outdone yourselves. The food looks amazing and smells even better."

Becky beamed. "Thank you, Shelby. Every bite was made with love."

Becky looked around her at the lighted tent, the flowers and candles, and all of the special touches.

"This is absolutely amazing, Shelby. I can't believe what you have done here. It looks like a picture in a magazine."

"I can't take credit for this one," Shelby replied, smiling. "This is a Lily Lane original. She was the Director of Operations. Yeardley and I were just her foot soldiers."

"Speaking of Yeardley," Jackson interrupted, "where is she?" He cast a wary glance around the lawn.

Shelby remembered what Yeardley had told her about Jackson and the cottage. She hated to think it was true. Shelby gave a nonchalant shrug.

"I think she's in the house getting ready. Aunt Nola's there too, with my parents." She looked at Jackson sternly. She hated doubting him. But if he was innocent and Yeardley was wrong then he had nothing to worry about walking into the lion's den.

Jackson nodded and moved toward the house, leaving his parents and Shelby to finish their conversation.

"You two need a glass of champagne. Let me show you to the bar." Shelby made sure Bob and Becky were settled enjoying a cocktail and the music before making her own way back to the house. It was time to bring out the guest of honor.

"Aunt Nola? Mom? Dad? It's time for the birthday girl to go to her party."

Nola and Natalie were in the living room. They sat side-by-side on the couch, heads bowed together, speaking softly. Nola looked peaceful. Natalie looked optimistic. Perhaps they had already come up with a plan to help Nola.

"Come on, girls. It's show time! Where's Dad?" Shelby asked.

"He's in the kitchen talking with Jackson." Natalie stood and placed a hand under Nola's elbow, escorting her sister to the door.

"Tell Dad we'll meet him out there."

Male voices greeted Shelby as she entered the kitchen wondering what carnage she might find. Her dad would never let anyone hurt his family. But there were no signs of trouble as her dad and Jackson bonded over beers.

"Come on, guys." Relieved, Shelby ushered the men out the door. "The party has started. We need you all out there."

Shelby shooed them out of the house. Ready to follow them, she had one last thing to take care of. On the counter, a leaning tower of manila folders threatened to topple over; Shelby's party planning files. Opening the top one, she pulled out a birthday card for Nola. The card was blank inside, waiting for Shelby to pen a personal message to Aunt Nola. Shelby chewed on the end of her pen, summoning the words to write.

Footsteps sounded behind her, and a warm hand placed itself gently on Shelby's shoulder.

"Dad, I'm coming. I just need to write this card for Aunt Nola." Turning in her seat, Shelby's mouth dropped open.

"Matt? Oh my God! What are you doing here? When did you get here? Are you okay?" Questions flew from Shelby's mouth in rapid succession.

Matt leaned down, kissing her firmly on the mouth. "I'm happy to see you, too." He laughed, hugging her tight. "But Shelby, we need to talk."

Holding Matt close, Shelby's smile dimmed and her heart began to race. "Matt, I am so sorry. You have to believe me. I don't even want to go to California if you're not with me. Even then I'm not so sure that's where I want to be."

Matt's hands rested lightly on her shoulders as he pulled back to look at her. Shelby thought he had never looked so handsome with one dark brow raised doubtfully and his mouth tipped in a teasing smile.

"I swear, Matt. This is our decision to make together."

Matt spoke, never taking his eyes off Shelby's face. "A lot has happened this week, Shel, to both of us. Can we talk, privately?"

Shelby's stomach was in knots. *What else had happened while she was away?* "Sure," she said, looking around the room, unable to meet his eyes. "The kitchen is kind of Grand Central today, but I'm sure we can find somewhere quiet."

Matt grabbed Shelby's hand. "I know just the place," he said, leading her out the door.

Shelby followed him, too numb to question where he was taking her or how he knew where to go. Walking briskly, Matt made his way across the front lawn, avoiding the tent and the clusters of people gathered to celebrate. Shelby followed, trotting behind him onto the dock, where a pair of Adirondack chairs nested together, white balloons and white crepe paper streaming from their backs. In front of them, an ice bucket with a bottle of champagne and two flutes beckoned the couple to sit.

"What is this?" Shelby was confused. "We didn't set this up."

"Lily did this for me," Matt said softly. He motioned for Shelby to take one of the chairs, joining her in the other.

"Lily? Why?"

Matt did not answer. Grabbing the bottle of champagne he popped it open, filling the flutes one at a time. Handing one to Shelby, he raised his own in a toast.

"To you, an amazing woman who can do anything she sets her mind to. I can't tell you how proud I am of you and excited for the opportunities your future holds."

Shelby's heart began to sink. Where was Matt going with this?

"Shelby, I think I've known since the day we met in the elevator that you are the love of my life. I adore you. You make me happier than I could ever have imagined." Placing his glass on the ground, Matt knelt before Shelby's chair.

"Whatever you decide about California is fine with me. I'll go wherever you go because you are my home."

Before Shelby could register what he had said, Matt reached into his pocket and pulled out a small box. He opened it, showing her a beautiful solitaire cut diamond.

"Shelby Marie Lane, will you be my wife?"

Shelby was stunned. "All I could think about was myself and what I wanted. I was so selfish and self-centered." Shaking her head, she said, "I thought that was why you stopped returning my calls." She looked at Matt in disbelief. "You're not breaking up with me?"

Matt's face turned red. "You know I can't keep a secret. I was afraid if we talked, I'd spill the beans about picking out the ring and planning the proposal. You're my best friend, Shelby. I tell you everything."

Matt's hand was shaky as he touched her cheek. A speechless Shelby stared at him. "Uh, Shelby, do you think you might have an answer? I'm kinda hanging here."

Tears of joy stung Shelby's eyes as she threw herself into Matt's arms. "Yes! Yes! Of course I'll marry you."

Pulling Shelby to her feet, Matt slipped the ring on her finger.

"I love you," they said in unison.

Sweeping Shelby off her feet, Matt spun her around to face the cottage. Raising his glass high, he yelled, "She said yes!"

Cheers erupted from the lawn where Shelby's family and friends had all gathered with champagne flutes in hand. Aunt Nola, her parents and sisters, Jackson and his parents, Mr. Murphy and Miss Jean. Suddenly shy, she buried her head in Matt's neck. She was engaged! Her hand sparkled with the setting sun as she admired her diamond ring. It was almost as beautiful as the man beside her.

The happy couple made their way back to shore to the sound of happy cheers and shouted congratulations. After a few minutes, Shelby waved her hands to quiet the growing crowd.

"Hey everyone! This was such an unbelievable surprise. All I can tell you is that I love this man with all my heart, and nothing means more to me than sharing this moment with all of you, my family and friends. I am one very lucky girl. Thank you all so much for your good wishes."

Gathering her sisters to her side, Shelby continued, "But today, we are here to celebrate a woman who is precious and so special to all of us. Aunt Nola, thank you for making our lives here at the lake magical. We love you. Happy Birthday."

Raising their glasses in the air, Shelby, Yeardley, and Lily proclaimed together, "Let the party begin!"

YEARDLEY

Jackson. The sight of him shook me to the core. The happy group that had gathered to congratulate Shelby and Matt had dispersed, leaving Jackson on his own, alone. I rushed to confront him, my cheeks flaming from the memory of our last encounter.

"I thought I made myself perfectly clear," I snapped, the words falling between us like broken twigs. Jackson started to speak but I wouldn't let him.

"You are not welcome here," I enunciated slowly and clearly.

Around us, the party was in full swing. From the dance floor, Mr. Murphy waved, beckoning us to join him, but neither of us moved. Jackson and I faced-off, still as statues, neither of us so much as blinking.

"Yeardley? Jackson?" Nola's voice, warm and concerned, broke through the impasse. In unison, we turned to face her.

"What's going on?"

Glancing from me to Jackson and back again, Nola's face was creased with worry. This was her party, and we were ruining it.

Correction, Jackson was ruining it. Why did he have to come? Guilt turned to anger, and I pointed at Jackson accusingly.

"I'm so sorry, Aunt Nola. I told him not to come." Staring hard at Jackson, I assured her, "He was just leaving, weren't you, Jackson?"

"Leaving? No!" Nola grabbed Jackson's arm, pressing him to stay. She stared at me aghast. "Yeardley, what are you doing?"

I was doing my best to protect her, but the look on Nola's face said I was failing miserably. I struggled to understand.

"Trust me, Aunt Nola. You don't want him here." Too disgusted to even look at Jackson, I thrust another accusing finger in his direction.

"He's a thief and a liar."

"WHAT?" The single word ripped through me as Jackson stepped close, grabbing my elbow. Squeezing it hard, he spoke through gritted teeth. "You don't know what the hell you're talking about."

"The hell I don't!" I spat back, wrenching my arm free from his grip. "And don't you dare touch me." Rubbing the injured party with my other hand, I turned to Nola and explained.

"I heard you on the phone with him, Aunt Nola. I know Jackson is taking the cottage away from you. He shouldn't be here. Not now. Not at your party."

We listened a moment to the music of the night; laughing voices, clinking glasses, and the lake lapping kisses on the shore.

The perfumed scent of a summer evening mingled with the aroma of tangy barbecue and sweet strawberries beneath the warm glow of twinkle lights and starlight. It was a perfect evening.

"Don't worry, Aunt Nola. I've got this under control." I smiled convincingly. "Go enjoy your party. I'll join you in a minute."

I forced myself to look at Jackson. Still flushed with anger, his nostrils flared like a bull in a ring, and I was the toreador, waving the red cape in front of him.

"Yeardley, sweetheart, I appreciate what you're trying to do, but you've got it all wrong."

Keeping one eye trained on Jackson, I let the other settle on Nola. "What do you mean?"

"Let's go sit down," Nola urged, nodding at Jackson. "All three of us. I'll explain everything."

We settled ourselves at one of the picnic tables scattered about the lawn for outdoor seating. Nola instructed Jackson and me to sit on one side, while she took the other. We sat without touching, staring stiffly at Nola.

"I'll never forget that day," Nola began. "At first, I didn't really understand what happened. I went to that coffee shop in Grandton. No one there had ever heard of Steven Fontaine. And then it hit me like a ton of bricks. I knew it was all gone.

Everything. All I could do was leave. I didn't feel anything, just numb."

"You were in shock," Jackson said quietly, reaching to hold Nola's hand.

Nola did not hear him. She continued.

"I got in my car and started to drive home. It was so quiet. Too quiet, and I started to think. I wondered what my parents and grandparents would say if they knew what I had done. How could I have been so stupid? Losing my life savings was bad enough, but what about the house? This house has meant everything to so many generations of Hamilton's. And now, it would all be gone, because of me. I was so ashamed."

Nola's eyes were glassy as she looked at us.

"It was the worst day of my life. When I was finally close to home, I started to cry. I was shaking so hard by then that I could barely drive. I may be stupid, but I had enough sense to pull over and stop the car. And that's where Jackson found me. Crying like a baby in my car, on the side of the road."

Poker-faced, Jackson shifted uncomfortably on the bench. Fighting the urge to slap him, I gripped the picnic bench tightly.

"Poor Jackson," Nola smiled sympathetically. "I must have given you quite a fright in my hysterical state."

Jackson shrugged, and Nola looked at me. "Don't let him fool you. I was a wreck. But he stayed with me. Just letting me babble at first, then helping me sort things through."

Breathing deeply, Nola continued. "He took me to the bank to see if there was anything I might have missed. We sat with Conrad Hopper and told him everything. Unfortunately, there was nothing that we could do. The check was cashed and the money long gone. If the equity loan couldn't be paid back, then I would lose the cottage. We considered asking your parents for help, but I didn't want to drag them into my mess. They have their own finances to contend with not to mention, some day, three weddings to pay for."

Nola's voice cracked with emotion. She took a sip of her drink and continued.

"It was Jackson's idea to bring you girls back this summer. He knew how much you girls loved it here. I wasn't sure at first, it might be too hard for all of us, but then I thought you should have a chance to say good-bye."

"We do love it. And you too!" I blurted without hesitation.

"Yes, you do," agreed Nola. "But I know now it will take more than love to keep this home safe."

I started to speak again, but Nola stopped me.

"Yeardley, Shelby and Matt have a life in New York, or maybe California. They have careers and a new home of their own. And now they're getting married. Their roots are already planted. Lily is the complete opposite. She's a fledgling teetering on the edge of her nest. She's desperate to test her wings and fly free. She's not in any position to settle down here."

"And me?" I was almost afraid to hear her answer. "What about me?"

Taking her hand from Jackson, Nola clasped mine instead, smiling softly. "Yeardley, honey, you belong here heart and soul. I think you know that. You've been searching a long time for a place to call your own. And you've found it. You're home. No matter what happens to the cottage, you belong here."

"But?" I asked, wishing there was more that I could do.

"But it isn't enough, I'm afraid. I need money, and lots of it."

Jackson interrupted. "That's where I come in," he said. "That's why I'm *buying* the cottage from Nola. You said so yourself, Greene's is a booming business. I can afford to do this for Nola."

Choosing to ignore him, I spoke only to Nola. "So that's it then. You're selling out to Jackson. There's no other way?"

A low steam whistle sounded beside me as Jackson exhaled. His color was fading from an angry red to a frustrated pink.

"Jesus, Yeardley. Do you really think I'm that much of an asshole? I love Nola. I would never do anything to hurt her." He had heard enough. Jackson stood to leave.

"Please," Nola rested her hand on Jackson's forearm urging him to stay. Reluctantly, he sat down again.

"It's true, Yeardley," Nola interjected before I could retort. "Jackson is literally my life saver."

"You girls are my family," Nola continued. "I love you as much as if you were my own daughters. Our summers together when you were all little were some of the happiest times of my life. And this week was special too, spending time with the lovely young women you've become. But it's clear to me that you each have your own paths to follow. I can't and I won't ask you to change direction for me."

I started to interrupt, but Nola cut me off.

"Jackson is the son I never had," she said simply.

They shared a smile as I looked on, and the giant knot of anger inside my stomach began to shrink, ever so slightly.

"Jackson was born and raised here. He belongs here, too," she said, looking pointedly at me. "He may not be blood, but he's family just the same. And he's offered to buy the cottage to keep it in the family. We're still working out the details, but thanks to Jackson, the cottage will never belong to strangers "

Slowly I began to understand. The pieces of the puzzle were coming together at last. My cheeks flushed with embarrassment before my hands could cover them. All the accusations and insults I had hurled at Jackson, every one a bull's-eye. I could never take them back. The giant knot was unraveling fast.

"So you're not stealing the cottage from Nola?" I squeaked, my throat bone dry.

Eyeing me warily, Jackson did not seem to notice. "No."

"And she's not going to be homeless?"

Rolling his eyes, he shifted a little closer. "No. Like Nola said, we haven't worked out all of the details yet, but Nola's going to be fine. Just look at her."

Across the table, Nola's seat was empty, but her easy laugh helped me spot her right away welcoming some late arriving guests.

Jackson and I sat in awkward silence. "Looks like some more people are here. I better go help Nola," I mumbled, swinging my legs to one side of the bench and pushing myself up from the table.

"Not a chance," Jackson grabbed my hand, forcing me to sit again. "You're not going anywhere until you explain to me what kind of idiotic thinking is going on in that head of yours?"

My jaw dropped. I shut it quickly, too embarrassed to look at him.

"In all the years I've known you, Yeardley, there's never been a day when I didn't like you. Until now."

Jackson combed a hand through his hair, letting out a deep breath as he did. He was mad, frustrated, and disappointed in me. That hurt more than anything.

"I'm not loving me so much right now either," I mumbled, not sure what to say. He was right. I had judged him without any solid evidence. I had declared him guilty without any chance of defending himself or proving me wrong.

"Is that an apology?" Jackson shook his head unconvinced. "You called me a liar and a thief. That's all you have to say to me?"

I shrugged, feeling the tears welling in my eyes. I looked into Jackson's green ones, filled with hurt and something even worse. Jackson didn't believe me. I had lost his trust. Without it, I was suddenly cold and I rubbed my arms for warmth.

"Oh, Jackson, I am so sorry. For doubting you and yelling at you, and hating you. I'm sorry for everything." Tears streamed down my face, and Jackson started to say something. Touching my fingers to his lips, I stopped him. "Jackson, you're my best friend, I don't want to lose you. Can you forgive me?"

Time stood still as I waited for Jackson to answer me. Refusing to take my eyes from his, I willed him to say yes. "Whatever it takes," I promised him, "I'll do it."

Emotions danced across Jackson's face; first light then dark shadows chasing each other as Jackson decided the fate of our relationship. "This will never work," he said at last. The agony of waiting for him to respond gave way to a fresh flood of pain. "I don't know how it can."

Jackson looked sad. Suddenly, he was a seventeen-year-old boy again, pouring his heart out to me. "I want to be with someone who believes in me as much as I do them, someone who trusts me. Someone who will meet me halfway and always stand beside me, no matter what." His voice trailing off, Jackson propped an elbow on the table and rested his head in the palm of his hand.

We were both quiet, lost in thought, as the moon hovered over us, protectively. In the orb's soft light, I saw the future. The golden waves of Jackson's hair turned to sterling silver, his rugged skin was a gentle shade of pale. His brilliant eyes gleamed back at me, shining as brightly as ever. This was a man I could spend my life with. Someone I could grow old with.

"I can do that," I promised, my voice strong and clear. It had taken me a while, but I finally knew exactly where I belonged.

A muscle twitched in Jackson's face pulling the corner of his mouth into my favorite smile. "I need some time to think about it," he said, keeping me in the dark. "Are you planning to be here for awhile?"

"Yeardley! Jackson!

They were all together, my parents, Nola, Shelby and Matt, and Lily. Dad was pouring champagne into flutes. Mom waved us over.

"Come on, we're having a family toast."

Jackson's eyes were fixed on me, like emerald question marks. Grabbing his hand, I pulled him off the bench. "I'll be here for as long as it takes."

EPILOGUE

"Rise and shine, sleepyhead." Jackson snuggled close to Yeardley, nuzzling her ear with his lips. "We're going to miss our plane."

Yeardley groaned and stretched, sending a reluctant wake-up call to her still slumbering muscles. Opening her eyes, she rolled toward Jackson, eager for her morning kiss.

"Wait. You're dressed already?" She pouted, her disappointment obvious.

Jackson chuckled. "I figured you could use the extra sleep, after last night."

"Hmmm." Yeardley stretched again, her limbs languid with the memory of their lovemaking. "Last night was amazing. And the night before that, and the night before that." She grinned. "Keep it up, and I'll stay here forever."

"That's the plan." Jackson kissed her tenderly. "But right now we've got to get a move on. We still have to pick up Nola, and our flight leaves in a few hours."

"Right." Giving Jackson a peck on the lips, Yeardley jumped out of bed and headed for the shower. Soapsuds slid down her back as she rinsed her hair, thinking about the day ahead of them. By this afternoon, she, Jackson, and Nola would all be in Boston. She could hardly wait.

Six months had passed since Nola's birthday party. Six months since Jackson had asked her to stay. Six months of working together every day at the market, and spending every night together, getting reacquainted. Her life was coming together at last. Only something really big could make Yeardley ever want to leave this place again. Shelby and Matt's wedding fit the bill.

At the baggage claim, Shelby and Matt waited, excited for her family to arrive. "I'm so happy that Yeardley and Lily were able to coordinate their arrival times," Shelby said, scanning the crowd for her sisters, and Nola and Jackson. "Four people, one pick up. Easy."

Matt squeezed Shelby's hand, smiling at her efficiency. Shelby smiled back, admiring the handsome man beside her. Tomorrow, he would be her husband. Shelby's smile widened at the thought. All her dreams were coming true.

"How do you feel about getting married in Boston?" she had asked him, already knowing his answer. She and Matt were traditionalists. They would be married in her hometown with her sisters as bridesmaids, and her father escorting her down the aisle of St. Mary's church. A black tie reception at the prestigious

Harvard Club would follow, thanks to some professional string pulling by her mother.

"The same way I feel about us staying in New York," he had answered without hesitation. "California. Colorado. Connecticut. It doesn't matter to me. Home is where you are."

Planting a kiss on Matt's cheek, Shelby wrapped her arms around his waist. "I love you too," she said. "California was a good deal but not sweet enough. I have everything I need right here; a nice promotion, our home, you." Shelby tilted her face to Matt's. "Besides, New York's closer to Connecticut and I hear that's a great place to raise kids. Some day." She winked.

Catching sight of Lily, Shelby jumped and waved enthusiastically, guiding her sister to where she and Matt were waiting.

"Lily! Over here."

Impeccably dressed in a winter white coat with a black cashmere scarf looped loosely around her neck, Lily looked like a native New Englander ready to take on January's frosty temps. Shelby looked surprised, and Lily laughed.

"Christmas gifts from Mom and Dad," she explained, twirling like a ballerina. "You like?"

Shelby and Matt nodded their approval and Lily hugged them both. "I have to admit, I like them too, even if they are a bit heavy for Miami."

Taking a step back, Lily ran a critical eye over her sister and soon-to-be brother-in-law. Wearing his-and-her matching parkas over turtleneck sweaters, jeans, and snow boots, they looked more like eskimoes than lovebirds.

"It's not too late you know," Lily remarked, drawing quizzical looks from the heavily layered couple. "To have the wedding in Florida, I mean. It was eighty-five degrees and sunny when I left this morning." She leaned close, her voice low and husky. "Nothing says romance like a little Miami heat."

Shelby shook her head and Matt laughed. "We're saving the heat for the honeymoon. A little thunder down under if you know what I mean?"

Shelby blushed as Lily nodded approvingly, wiggling her eyebrows at Matt. "That's what I'm talking about, McSteamy."

Eager to change the subject, Shelby asked, "Speaking of hot and steamy, Lily, how're things with Diego?"

"Good." Lily's response was automatic. She paused to think. It was a different girl who had returned to Miami from a week in Shepardsville. She knew it, and Diego had known it too.

Meeting Lily at the gate with the world's largest bouquet of roses in one arm, and a red velvet box in his hand, Diego had immediately scooped her into his protective embrace.

"Mi preciosa, my precious. I missed you," he breathed warmly in her ear.

Diego's arms trapped her like a net. Lily willed herself to relax. Once upon a time, she had thrived on his devotion. It made her feel like a princess in a fairy tale, Diego showering her with gifts and adoring accolades. "The fairest one in all of Miami," he would say, proudly showing her off to his clients, his friends, to Miami's elegant elite. It was surreal, flattering, and safe. But it was not enough for her anymore.

Lily wasn't exactly sure when it had happened, or how, but sometime during her visit to the lake, she had changed. Princess Lily had disappeared and in her place, Lily Lane had stepped forward. It was a new world for her, out from under Diego's attentive hovering, and her family's, too, all of them busy with their own affairs. Shelby, Yeardley, and Nola had left the baby of the family to fend for herself at last.

Relishing her newfound freedom and all that came with it, Lily had put every ounce of creative skill she had into designing a spectacular party for Nola. One she would never forget, Lily promised, as she focused on turning concept into reality. Like a master puppeteer, she had worked, pulling, pushing, and tugging everything into its proper place. Managing every detail, big and small, with a competence and confidence she never knew she had, Lily had surprised herself. Diego would be proud too, she thought.

As if she had said his name out loud, Diego held her gently at arm's length. "Is something wrong, bella?" He eyed her appreciatively, from head to toe. "You seem different."

Lily nodded, agreeing with him. She had seen it too, facing off with her reflection in the mirror that morning. The differences were subtle, but palpable. Her eyes were brighter, clear and crisp as an autumn sky. In profile, the soft lines of her chin and jaw were sharp with determination. And her lips, always rosy and quick to smile, were fully pronounced as if she had something really important to say.

"Diego, we need to talk."

From the airport to Diego's apartment, Lily talked while Diego listened. "I need this, Diego," she explained, searching his face for understanding. "I need something of my own, and I need to do it myself."

Lily took a deep breath and continued. "My whole life I've been taken care of by other people, my family, my friends, you." Taking Diego's hand in hers, she smiled. "Don't get me wrong, I'm grateful. But at some point, everyone has to grow up. I can do it. But I need your help."

"Lily Lane: Custom Creations for the Stars." Diego mulled over her proposal. "A niche division of Alvarez Designs that caters to the younger generation of celebrity artists and athletes?"

Lily nodded affirmatively. "It takes youth to know what youth likes. And it takes experience to know how to upsell the target market. My age is my own and you have already given me some experience, Diego, but you have so much more to share. Believe me, with a little help, I can make this work, for both of us. What do you say?"

Several weeks later, *Lily Lane* was born, though not soon enough for the company's namesake. Eager to get started, Lily had wanted to jump right in, but Diego refused, insisting they run market assessment reports and financials first.

"Success does not come from rushing in willy-nilly," he reminded her.

"Which is exactly why we need each other," Lily assured him.

Diego was still struggling with the new status of their relationship. No longer lovers, they were strictly business partners now. Lily was one hundred percent committed to her career.

"I have to give it my best shot, or nothing at all," she explained, praying Diego would stand by her professionally.

Diego's business acumen was the perfect counterpart to her creative energies. Teaching her how to make decisions based on fact rather than emotion, he had created a rock solid foundation for Lily's inspired undertaking. And their partnership was working. Lily Lane was quickly becoming the go-to designer for Miami's young celebrities.

Smiling to herself, Lily focused her attention on Shelby. "We're both really good," she said.

"Shelby! Lily!" Nola emerged suddenly from the swirling crowd of winter coats and suitcases. Yeardley and Jackson were right behind her.

Taking stock of her group, Shelby counted heads making sure they were all present and accounted for. "Okay everyone," she said, raising her voice over the dull roar of the baggage claim. "Let's get this wedding weekend started!"

At the rehearsal dinner that evening, Nola caught Natalie's eye, motioning to her sister to join her at the bar in the corner of the private dining room.

"Thanks," said Natalie, gratefully accepting the proffered cocktail: an extra dirty martini with extra olives. "Just the way I like it," she sighed happily.

Nola smiled, watching with amusement as Natalie discreetly removed her heels, flexing the cramps from her sorely pinched feet.

"Who knew being mother-of-the-bride would hurt so much?"

Glancing around the room, Natalie spotted each of her girls; Shelby and Matt, arms linked, were making the rounds among their guests. Lily, her blonde hair cascading over her shoulders, sparkled like a diamond in a ring of male admirers. It took her a moment longer to find Yeardley. Standing with Jackson, his arm draped lightly across her shoulders, they were a united front fielding questions from curious relatives and friends.

"How long do you think before I have to put these heels on again?" Natalie asked Nola, lifting her chin in Yeardley's direction.

Nola laughed. "If I were a betting girl, I'd gamble everything I had on it not being long now." She grew somber. "But I guess I already did that."

"Hey." Natalie grabbed her sister's hand tightly, no longer talking about Yeardley. "Nola, you thought you were doing the right thing. You made a mistake. And then you fixed it. When is Jackson going to move in anyway?"

Nola had been wondering the same thing. The papers were signed months ago. The house belonged to Jackson now. But he had encouraged Nola to stay on as long as she liked.

"I've got my own place, and it's enough for me right now," Jackson had said after dinner one night. Nola had invited him over to discuss his timetable for moving from his house into the cottage. From the dining room, they could see Yeardley in the kitchen serving up slices of pie for dessert. Raspberry. Her favorite. Glancing up from her task, Yeardley had spotted Jackson, and smiled.

Beaming in response, Jackson had winked at Nola and said, "Besides, I have an ulterior motive."

After Nola's party, Yeardley had stayed on with her. "Who knows what will happen with Jackson," she told Nola. "All I know for sure is that I've never felt more at home than I do here. Can I stay with you a while? I can help you with all the cottage stuff."

Remembering Yeardley's plea, Nola sipped her wine, masking the gentle snort that escaped her. Despite her niece's promises, Nola had barely seen Yeardley since Becky and Bob had hired her to work at the market. Yeardley had been spending all her days there with Jackson, and her nights with him too. Jackson's ulterior motive was becoming crystal clear.

Nola was happy for them. Yeardley and Jackson made a good team. Knowing the cottage would be safe in their hands, Nola was sleeping better than she had in a long time. Best of all, she was ready to chart a new course for herself.

"Are you nervous?" Natalie asked, reading Nola's mind as she chewed thoughtfully on an olive.

"Excited is more like it."

It hadn't taken long for word of Nola's troubles to spread through Shepardsville. After the party, it seemed to Nola as if every single one of her friends and neighbors, had stopped by to see how they could help. They brought everything from casseroles to cash, which Nola had graciously refused.

"I am so touched, but really I can't and I don't need to. Jackson's got it all under control," she said gratefully.

But one offer was too good to refuse. "Nola, you're perfect for the job," Kathleen Cavendish was convinced. "You're an experienced library administrator, you're a wonderful teacher at the Adult Exchange. There's no way you could be anything but the perfect adjunct at Canandaigua Community College."

Nola wasn't as sure but she was game to try. Teaching at night would add a new dimension to her already full life.

"I'm more than ready. Oh, Natalie, I am so ready for it all."

"And what about the cottage?"

Nola understood at once what Natalie was asking. She nodded at Yeardley and Jackson. "Eventually, those two are going to need a bigger place than Jackson's, if you catch my drift, Grandma." She teased Natalie, poking her gently in the ribs. "We can swap houses whenever they're ready."

"What are you two whispering about over here?" Shelby, Yeardley, and Lily joined the two women, eyeing them with suspicion.

"Conspiring about something, I'm sure," Yeardley observed dryly, sipping from her mother's martini before passing it to Lily.

"Be afraid," added Lily accepting the glass from her sister. "Be very afraid."

"It's true. Nothing good can come from that," Shelby shuddered. "Remember the time Mom and Nola thought we'd all look cute with pageboy hair cuts?"

"I looked like Shep from the Three Stooges," Yeardley groaned.

"Better than The Little Dutch Boy," Lily countered, taking no joy from trumping her sister.

"Enough!" Natalie and Nola wiped tears of laughter from their eyes.

"So we made a few mistakes," Nola admitted.

"But not too many, I think," said Natalie, smiling affectionately at her daughters.

"You're The Pie Sisters after all! What's sweeter than that?"

# # #

The Pie Sisters

244

About the Authors

Friends Leigh Brown and Victoria Corliss became co-authors in 2009. In 2013, they published their first novel, *Second Chances* as an e-book, later releasing it in paperback.

Active speakers and book event participants, they are often asked: 1) Are they sisters, and 2) How do they write books together? They are sisters in spirit only. To learn how their collaboration works, visit their website at http://www.browncorlissbooks.com, or invite them to speak to your book club. Contact them at browncorlissbooks@gmail.com.

Paperback and e-copies of *The Pie Sisters* and *Second Chances* are available at http://www.amazon.com and www.smashwords.com.

Made in the USA
Middletown, DE
13 March 2015